PUFFIN BOOKS

THE PUFFIN BOOK OF
SCHOOL STORIES

Bernard Ashley has had a long career in the teaching profession.
As a young teacher in Kent he taught children with special learning difficulties, and it was from this experience that he saw the
need for direct reading matter which would interest older children, so he began writing his own books. He lives in Charlton,
South London, not far from the scenes of his early childhood,
teaching and writing books for children of all ages, picture books
to teenage novels, as well as being a busy television writer.

Also in this series

The Puffin Book of

School STORIES

Chosen by

Bernard Ashley

Illustrations by Stephen Lee

PUFFIN BOOKS

PUFFIN BOOKS

Published by the Penguin Group
Penguin Books Ltd, 27 Wrights Lane, London W8 5TZ, England
Penguin Books USA Inc., 375 Hudson Street, New York, New York 10014, USA
Penguin Books Australia Ltd, Ringwood, Victoria, Australia
Penguin Books Canada Ltd, 10 Alcorn Avenue, Toronto, Ontario, Canada M4V 3B2
Penguin Books (NZ) Ltd, 182–190 Wairau Road, Auckland 10, New Zealand

Penguin Books Ltd, Registered Offices: Harmondsworth, Middlesex, England

First published by Viking 1992
Published in Puffin Books 1993
3 5 7 9 10 8 6 4

This selection copyright © Bernard Ashley, 1992
Illustrations copyright © Stephen Lee, 1992
All rights reserved

The acknowledgements on pages 183–184 constitute an extension
to this copyright page

The moral right of the authors has been asserted

Printed in England by Clays Ltd, St Ives plc
Filmset in Lasercomp Bembo

Contents

Introduction

I grew up mainly in south London but also in
various other parts of England; our home was in
Woolwich, on the Thames, but in the Second World
War we were evacuated to Staplehurst in Kent, to
Preston in Lancashire and to Worthing in Sussex, each
at a different stage of the bombing. I went to fourteen
different primary schools − including some in places I
can't remember − and nowhere did I come across a
school story which was about a school like any of
them. Perhaps it would have been unreasonable to
expect anyone to write a story about a contemporary
Elementary School while the war was going on (things
were happening too fast), but no one wrote about
Elementary Schools anyway − in those days they
weren't the 'stuff' for books. No one bothered looking
for stories of ordinary schools because no one expected

Introduction

them to have been written: books *weren't* about kids like us. If we wanted to read stories about children at school (and they would be about boys in a boys' school or girls in a girls' school), then we got hold of comics or books which were set in fee-paying public schools. The boys I read about didn't go home at the end of the afternoon, they went to their school Houses, where, instead of doing homework, they did prep; and at the end of term there were no school holidays for them, but vacations. And we identified with these remote characters and went around talking about doing our prep and having vacations – generally feeling inferior – because there was no alternative.

But we have a need to see ourselves written about. We need to understand by reading the adventures of fictitious characters that the sorts of things that happen to us have happened to others, that someone (if only the author) understands. We need to know that we're not the only one who has come up against this problem or that, who has had to make certain choices. It's comforting to know that others wet the bed, have been offered cigarettes or drink or perhaps drugs, that families have split up, that people outside ourselves can feel isolated, or fall hopelessly in love.

It's different now. Since my school-days, when the library collection was thirty thick volumes on a classroom shelf (and we had to read them in order: *Masterman Ready, Treasure Island, The Children of the New*

2

Forest, Little Women, Little Men . . .), we now have school libraries to rival the public ones, and as many modern school stories as we could wish for; some of them, thank goodness, reflecting the lives of all the various groupings in our society. To talk of *the* school story would be a mistake. As well as schools for older and younger pupils there are still public schools, all sorts of state schools, and specialist schools which teach singing and acting and ballet; while through film and television we know something of schools abroad.

In this collection I have ranged across the years and the schools and the Atlantic, appealing, I hope, to many readers who might be looking for themselves – in this generation, and in the generations of times past.

Bernard Ashley

Jam for Bunter!

FRANK RICHARDS

Billy Bunter, portrayed in comics and in books, is probably the most famous of all public-school characters. Tom Brown, of *Tom Brown's School-days* is a more serious character and the book is more generally admired, but there were many more Bunter adventures to read about, and they were immensely popular in the way that Roald Dahl's books became later. What is striking in reading the Bunter stories now is how a disability like being fat was made fun of by the author, and how unusual it was for a boy of Asian origin (Hurree Jamset Ram Singh) to be in a British school: so that Frank Richards had to invent a sort of 'funny' English for him to speak. And there were canings in every chapter, all

5

intended to be laughed at, given by teachers who seemed hardly human.

In this extract from *Billy Bunter of Greyfriars School*, published in 1947, Bunter has, as usual, been accused of stealing someone's food . . .

'Stand and deliver!'

'Oh, really, Cherry – !'

'What have you got there?'

'Nothing, old chap! Nothing at all! I say, you fellows, let a fellow pass. I'm in rather a hurry.'

But the Famous Five, of the Remove, did not let Billy Bunter pass.

They were coming upstairs as Billy Bunter came down. They met on the middle landing. Five fellows, in a grinning row, blocked Billy Bunter's way to the lower staircase. Bunter halted unwillingly – but he had to halt.

That Billy Bunter had something hidden under his jacket was a fact that leaped to the eye. Bunter's garments were tight. There was really hardly enough room in them for Bunter. His ample proportions filled them almost to bursting point. Any other fellow might have concealed something under his jacket without catching the casual eye. Not Bunter. On Bunter's fat person there was a bulge – a very distinct bulge – a bulge that few could have failed to notice. Harry Wharton and Co. had noticed it at once. That was

why Bob Cherry playfully called on the fat junior to
stand and deliver.

Bunter was clearly in a hurry. Bunter's movements
generally resembled those of a snail – a tired snail. But
he had come pattering rapidly down the upper stairs,
and he came across the middle landing at a run. Only
for very urgent reasons could the fat Owl of the
Remove have put on such speed. But hurried as he
was, Bunter had to stop.

'I say, you fellows, no larks!' gasped Bunter. 'I –
I've got to see Quelch. He's waiting to see me. Let a
chap pass.'

'You've got to see Quelch?' repeated Harry Wharton.

'Yes, old chap – he's waiting –'

'How odd, we've just seen Quelch go out. You've
missed him,' said the captain of the Remove, shaking
his head.

'Oh! Has Quelch gone out? I – I don't mean
Quelch! I – I mean Wingate,' stammered Bunter. 'I've
got to see Wingate! Let a chap pass – can't keep a
Sixth-form prefect waiting – captain of the school,
too! I've got to get to Wingate's study –'

'No good going to his study,' chuckled Frank
Nugent. 'Wingate's on Big Side, playing cricket.'

'Oh! Is he? I mean – I – I – I mean – I mean the
Head! That's what I – I meant to say. I've been
specially sent for to Dr Locke's study. I say, you

fellows, I shall get into a row if I keep the Headmaster waiting! You know old Locke doesn't like to be kept waiting – lemme pass, will you?'

And Billy Bunter made an effort to push through the row of juniors. Then he gave a startled yelp, as the bulge under his jacket slipped. He clutched wildly at the hidden article to save it, and crammed it back under his jacket – but not before the other fellows had seen that it was a jam-jar.

'Ha, ha, ha!' roared Bob Cherry. 'Are you taking the Head a pot of jam for his tea?'

'Oh! Yes! No! I – I –'

'Whose is it?' asked Johnny Bull.

'Mine!' roared Bunter indignantly. 'Think I've got somebody else's pot of jam? Not that this is a pot of jam I've got here, you know. It's a – a bottle of ink.'

'Smithy had jam in one of his gorgeous parcels today!' remarked Bob Cherry. 'You fat brigand, that's Smithy's jam.'

''Tain't!' roared Bunter. 'Think I'd touch Smithy's jam? I never knew Smithy had jam – I never saw Gosling hand him the parcel, and never knew he had a parcel at all, and it certainly wasn't in his study when I looked. Besides, I haven't been to his study. Will you let a fellow pass? I've got to see Quelch – I mean Wingate – that is, the Head – they're waiting – I mean, he's waiting – I mean –'

'Hallo, hallo, hallo!' roared Bob Cherry, as another

junior appeared on the lower staircase, coming up. 'This way, Smithy, old man.'

Herbert Vernon-Smith glanced up at the group on the middle landing.

'What's up?' he asked.

'Daylight raid!' answered Bob. 'If you had a pot of jam in your study, you'd better cut along and see if it's still there.'

'What?' Smithy joined the group on the middle landing, and his eye went at once to the bulge under Bunter's jacket. 'You fat villain! Have you been bagging my jam?'

'No!' gasped Bunter. 'I haven't got anything under my jacket, Smithy – I mean, it's a bottle of ink. I'm taking it down to the Rag, to – to fill the ink-pot. I say, you fellows, let a fellow pass.'

'If you've bagged my plum jam – !'

'I – I haven't, old chap! This bottle of ink is apricot jam – I – I mean, this jar of apricot is ink bottle – I – I mean –' Billy Bunter was getting a little mixed. 'Look here, you cut along to your study, Smithy, and you'll see your jar of jam on the table, just where you left it. You fellows go with him – !'

'Ha, ha, ha!'

'I'm just taking this bottle of jam down to the Rag to fill Quelch – I – I mean, I'm taking this jar of rag down to Quelch to see the Head. Ow! Leggo my neck, you beast!' howled Bunter, as the Bounder of

Greyfriars grasped him. 'I tell you I haven't got your jam. I don't believe you had any jam. There wasn't any in your study when I looked, and I left it on the table, too, just as it was — never touched it. If you can't take a fellow's word. Leggo!'

Shake! Shake! Shake!

Vernon-Smith had a sinewy arm. He shook Bunter, and shook him again and again, and the fat Owl sagged in his grasp, like a plump jelly. He clasped his fat hands over the bulge in his jacket to keep the hidden loot from slipping out. Even Billy Bunter realized that if that jar of plum jam came to light, nobody would believe his statement that it was a bottle of ink.

Shake! Shake!

'Ooooogh!' spluttered Bunter. 'Leggo! I say, you fellows, make him leggo! I say, you make him leggo, and I'll let you have some of the jam!'

'Ha, ha, ha!'

Shake! Shake! Shake!

Smithy, grinning, put his beef into it. The fat Owl tottered in his grasp, gurgling for breath. There was a sudden bump, as the jar of jam slipped, at last, from under Bunter's jacket, and rolled on the landing. Bunter's plunder had been shaken out of him and was revealed, to all eyes, as a pot of plum jam.

'Looks more like jam than ink to me!' remarked Nugent.

'The jamfulness is terrific!' grinned Hurree Jamset Ram Singh. 'The esteemed and execrable Bunter has been study-raiding.'

'Ow! I haven't!' gasped Bunter. 'That's my jam! It came from Bunter Court this morning! You leave my jam alone.'

Herbert Vernon-Smith, releasing the fat Owl, stooped to pick up his pot of jam. Billy Bunter made a dive for it. There was a sudden crash, as two heads suddenly met. Vernon-Smith gave a yell of anguish, and sat down suddenly on the landing. Bunter reeled from the shock.

'Ha, ha, ha!' shrieked the Famous Five.

'Oh, scissors!' gasped the Bounder. He sat with his hand to his head, dizzy from the crash. For a moment or two, he was *hors de combat*.

Billy Bunter did not lose that moment or two. His bullet head was harder than Smithy's, apparently. Perhaps there was not much in it to damage. Bunter clutched up the disputed pot of jam, and jumped for the lower stairs. Harry Wharton and Co. were laughing too much to stop him. Bunter went down the staircase with leaps like a kangaroo.

'Ha, ha, ha!'

Vernon-Smith staggered to his feet, his hand still to his head. His face was red with wrath.

'By gum! I'll burst him all over Greyfriars!' he gasped. And he rushed in pursuit of the fleeing fat Owl.

'Hold on, Smithy!' gasped Harry Wharton. But the enraged Bounder did not heed. Bunter had reached the foot of the staircase, and Smithy shot down in pursuit. The Owl of the Remove cast one terrified blink back, and fled for his fat life. The look on Smithy's face was enough for Bunter.

'Oh, my hat!' gurgled Bob Cherry. 'If they run into a beak or a pre., there will be a row.'

Smithy with his usual recklessness, was not thinking of masters or prefects. Neither was he bothering about the jam. With a bump on his head, and a pain therein, he just wanted to get hold of Billy Bunter.

Bunter, on the other hand, did not want to be got hold of. He had to get away from Smithy – and he remembered, as he careered away, that Wharton had mentioned that Quelch had gone out. Quelch's study, therefore, was a safe retreat – even the reckless Bounder would not venture to pursue him into a master's study. At a less hectic moment, the fat Owl would have thought twice, or three times, before he ventured into such dangerous precincts. But it was now a case of any port in a storm – and Billy Bunter flew for Quelch's study like a homing pigeon.

Smithy charged into Masters' passage, just in time to hear Quelch's study door slam ahead of him. Mr Prout, the master of the Fifth Form, looked out of his study doorway, and fixed his eyes with grim disapproval on the breathless, crimson Bounder.

'Well,' he rapped. 'What do you want here, Vernon-Smith?'

Smithy backed round the corner without replying to that question. Billy Bunter had found a safe refuge, and Vernon-Smith had to leave him to it. His only consolation was to resolve to burst William George Bunter all over Greyfriars School when he saw him again.

Mr Quelch stared, as if he could hardly believe his eyes.

Indeed, at that moment, he hardly could.

Quelch had gone out for a walk in the quad after class, as he often did. Harry Wharton and Co. had in fact seen their form-master go out, as Wharton had mentioned to Bunter. But he had come in again.

It was very pleasant taking the air under the shady old branches of the ancient Greyfriars elms. It braced Quelch, after his labours in the Remove room with a numerous and slightly troublesome form. But on Quelch's study table lay a pile of form papers that had to be corrected, and Henry Samuel Quelch never forgot his duties. So, reluctantly but dutifully, Quelch at length retraced his steps to the House – and came to his study.

Naturally, he did not expect to find that study occupied. Least of all would he have expected it to be occupied by a fat junior with a pot of jam. But that was how he found it. He opened the study door, and was about to enter, when he stopped dead, his eyes fixed on a fat figure in his armchair. Quelch's eyes were very keen – often compared, in his form, to gimlets. But at that moment he really doubted their evidence.

Billy Bunter did not, for the moment, see his form-master. Bunter was busy.

Bunter had sought that safe refuge simply to escape from the wrathful Smithy. He had judged rightly – Smithy had not ventured to pursue him there. He was safe – till Quelch came in. Bunter was going to stay in that study as long as he possibly could: for the double purpose of keeping out of Smithy's way, and giving Smithy time to cool down and get over his temper. When Quelch came in, he was going to account for his presence there by asking Quelch a history question, as if he had come to the study for that very purpose. That, Bunter sagely considered, would placate Quelch. Quelch, like all beaks, liked fellows to take an interest in their lessons: and he could not fail to be pleased if Bunter specially desired to know whether Magna Charta was signed in the reign of Edward the Confessor or Charles the Second!

In the mean time, there was the jam!

Billy Bunter liked jam. In fact, he loved it, with a faithful and abiding love. But the course of true love never did run smooth. Bunter did not meet the object of his affection nearly so often as he wished. So it was quite a windfall for Bunter when Smithy had that gorgeous parcel from home.

Sitting in Mr Quelch's armchair, Bunter opened that pot of jam. Unluckily he had no spoon. Bunter liked a tablespoon when dealing with jam. But on Quelch's table lay an ivory paper-knife which answered the purpose fairly well. With that implement, Billy Bunter scooped out jam and conveyed it to a large mouth: and chunk after chunk of delicious plum jam followed the downward path. In those ecstatic moments Bunter forgot Smithy, and even forgot Quelch. It was a happy, sticky Bunter that cleaned out the jam-jar with the ivory paper-knife.

After he had finished, Bunter was going to wipe that paper-knife clean on Quelch's blotting-pad, and hide the empty jam-jar at the bottom of Quelch's waste-paper basket – and then wait for Quelch, with his history question all ready. That was the idea. It was rather unfortunate that Quelch came in before Bunter had quite finished the jam!

There was still a spot of jam at the bottom of the jar, and it was not easy to extract it with a paper-knife. But difficulties were only made to be overcome. Bunter concentrated on that urgent task, blinking through his big spectacles into the jar resting on his fat knees, and scraping industriously. He was too absorbed to notice the faint sound of the door-handle turning.

As Mr Quelch stood at the open door, his eyes fixed on Bunter, the Owl of the Remove did not look up – he carried on with the important task in hand – and his little round eyes gleamed behind his big round spectacles, as quite a substantial spot of jam was gathered by industrious scraping.

Mr Quelch gazed at him.

For a long, long moment, the Remove master stood quite still, gazing at that happy member of his form. He realized that his eyes were not deceiving him. Actually a boy of his form was seated in his armchair in his study, scraping out a jam-jar, with a sticky paper-knife, sticky fingers, sticky face, and a general aspect of stickiness. Quelch found his voice.

'Bunter!'

'Oh, crikey!'

Bunter jumped. In fact, he bounded. He was out of the armchair with a speed that was marvellous, considering the weight he had to lift. The jam-jar rolled on the hearthrug. The sticky paper-knife dropped on the carpet. Billy Bunter stood blinking at his form-master with his eyes almost popping with terror through his spectacles.

'Bunter! What are you doing here?'

'Oh! I – I – I was – was waiting for you, sir!' gasped Bunter. 'I – I came to ask you a – a question, sir, about jam – I mean about history, sir – I – I forgot whether Magna Charta was signed by Smithy – I mean King Charles the Fourth, sir, or – or Henry the Tenth –'

'I find you eating – I should say devouring – I find you devouring jam, in my study!' said Mr Quelch, in a deep rumbling voice. 'Did you purloin that jam below stairs, Bunter? I have several times received complaints from Mrs Kebble –'

'Oh! No, sir! I – I had it in a parcel from home, sir! Smithy got it this morning – I mean, I got it this morning –'

'I think I understand, Bunter! You have purloined that comestible from another Remove boy's study, and that is why – !'

'Oh, no, sir! It wasn't Smithy's!' stammered Bunter. 'That was all a mistake, sir. If Smithy had any jam, it's still in his study. I – I didn't come here because Smithy was after me, sir – I – I came to ask you, sir, to tell me, if you'll be so kind, whether Cagna Marta – I mean Magna Charta – was signed in the reign of George the Seventh or – or – or William the Eighth, sir.'

'That will do, Bunter.'

'Yes, sir! Thank you, sir. C-c-can I go now, sir?'

'You may not, Bunter.'

'Oh, lor'!'

'I hardly know how to deal with you, Bunter,' said Mr Quelch, with slow, grim thoughtfulness. 'You are not only the idlest boy in my form. You are not only the most obtuse. You are the most untruthful. You are the most unscrupulous. You have been punished on several occasions for purloining food. Punishment appears to have no effect. You seem no better for even a severe caning.'

'Oh, no, sir!' gasped Bunter. 'Not at all, sir! Worse, I – I think, sir. I – I d–don't think caning does me any good, sir.'

'Once already this term, Bunter, you have been caned for taking a pie from the pantry –'

'That was all a mistake, sir!' groaned Bunter. 'I – I never went down the kitchen stairs at all. Mrs Kebble thought I'd gone down, sir, just because she saw me coming up –'

'On that occasion, Bunter, I gave you three strokes with the cane. It has not caused you to mend your ways,' said Mr Quelch. 'I shall not give you three strokes now, Bunter.'

'Oh! Good! I – I mean, thank you, sir. C–c–can I go now?'

'I shall give you six –!'

'Oh, crumbs!'

Mr Quelch picked up a cane from the study table. Billy Bunter eyed that proceeding with deep apprehension. Mr Quelch pointed to a chair with the cane.

'Bend over that chair, Bunter.'

'I – I – I say, sir –!'

'Bend over that chair!' rapped Mr Quelch, in a voice like unto that of the Great Huge Bear.

'Oh, crikey!'

Billy Bunter, in the lowest spirits, bent over the chair. He gave an anticipatory wriggle as he waited for the descending cane. But he did not have to wait long.

Swipe!

'Yarooooooh!' roared Bunter.

Swipe!

'Oh! Oooooh!'

Swipe! Swipe! Swipe!

'Yow-ow-whooooooooooop!'

SWIPE! Mr Quelch seemed to put extra beef in the last swipe. It fairly rang on Bunter's tight trousers. It cracked like a rifle-shot! Louder still sounded the anguished yell of the hapless Owl.

'Yow-ow-ow-ow-ow-ow!'

'Cease that ridiculous noise, Bunter,' snapped Mr Quelch.

'Yow-ow-ow-ow-ow!'

'If you make another sound, Bunter, I shall cane you again!'

Sudden silence!

'Now leave my study,' said Mr Quelch, 'and I warn you, Bunter, to let this be a lesson to you. I warn you that you have very nearly exhausted my patience. Go!'

Billy Bunter went.

He suppressed his feelings till Quelch's door closed

on him. But as he went wriggling down the passage, his anguish found voice.

'Yow-ow-ow-ow-ow-ow!'

'Oh! Here you are!' Herbert Vernon-Smith was waiting for him at the corner. 'Now, you fat villain – !'

'Yow-ow-ow-ow-ow-ow!'

The Bounder stared at him, dropped the foot he had lifted, and laughed.

'You look as if you've had enough!' he remarked.

'Yow-ow-ow-ow-ow-ow!'

Bunter certainly looked as if he had had enough. He felt as if he had had too much! And the Bounder kindly let it go at that, and Billy Bunter wriggled on his way unkicked.

Madame Fidolia and the Dancing Class

NOEL STREATFEILD

In contrast to looking for a story drawn from a life like our own we can go looking for escape – always an attractive idea, especially when we allow ourselves into a book's idyllic landscape by pretending to be the main character. The majority of people who enjoy pony stories don't own – or even ride – a pony, and the *Chalet School* stories are still being bought by people who have never been to Switzerland. But that doesn't dampen the desire to escape, to enjoy a feeling of holiday, of release: and its great advantage, being in a book, is that it need only be the turn of a page away.

For those who dream, then, as well as for those who dance, here is part of a ballet school story – perhaps the most famous ever

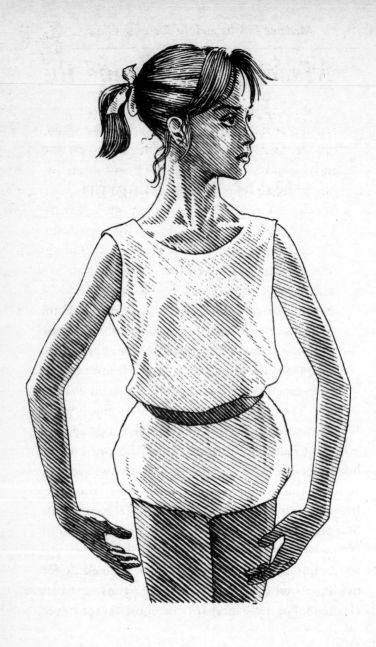

written: Noel Streatfeild's *Ballet Shoes* from 1936.

Pauline, Petrova and Posy are three orphans, rescued at different times by the fossil-collecting Professor Matthew Brown when on his travels, and brought up as the Fossil sisters by his great-niece Sylvia in a large house in London's Cromwell Road. But while Great-Uncle Matthew (Gum) is away, Sylvia falls on difficult times. She takes in boarders, including Mr and Mrs Simpson and Theo Dane, an instructress of dancing at the Children's Academy of Dancing and Stage Training: and when the question of schooling for the girls becomes a problem, Theo persuades Madame Fidolia – who owns the Academy – to take them on for free.

The Children's Academy of Dancing and Stage Training was in Bloomsbury. It was three large houses joined inside by passages. Across the front was written in large gold letters: 'Children's Acad' on the first house, 'emy of Dancing an' on the second, and 'd Stage Training' on the third. Theo had arranged that Nana and Sylvia should take the children round to see the place and to meet Madame Fidolia on a Wednesday afternoon, and that they should start their classes on the following Monday. Since it was a very important occasion, Mr Simpson said he would drive them all to the Academy in his car. The afternoon started badly. Pauline wanted to wear a party frock, which she said was the right thing for a dancing class; Nana, after discussion with Theo, had ironed and washed their blue-linen smocks and knickers.

'I want to wear our muslins,' said Pauline. 'At Cromwell House girls who learned dancing wore best frocks.'

'Only for ballroom dancing,' Petrova argued. 'They wore silk tunics for everything else; we haven't got those.'

Nana was firm.

'It's not a matter of what you've got or haven't got; you're putting on the smocks and knickers I've laid on your beds, so get on with changing while I dress Posy.'

'Why can't we wear our muslins?' Pauline growled.

'Because for the exercises and what they're going to see you do Miss Dane said plain cotton frocks and knickers. When you start on Monday you're having rompers, two each, black-patent ankle-strap shoes, and white tarlatan dresses, two each, with white sandal shoes, and white knickers, two pairs, all frills; so don't worry me, because I'm going to have worries enough getting all that lot made by Monday.'

Petrova pulled off her pink check frock and knickers, and got into the clean ones.

'What do we want all those for?'

Nana sighed.

'Ask me, dear! What we've got would do quite well for dancing in, I should say; but there's a printed list come, and there's all that on it, not to mention two rough face-towels for each child, clearly marked, and two special overalls to be bought through the school. Now you know. Come here, Pauline, and let me see to your hair.'

Petrova hurried through her dressing and ran downstairs. She found Mr Simpson sitting in his car.

'Hullo!' he called. 'Come beside me.' She scrambled in. He looked down at her and smiled. 'So they are going to train you as a dancer, are they?'

'Yes.' Petrova sighed. 'And I don't want to be one.'

'Why? Might be fun.'

'Not for me; I'm not any good. At Cromwell House we did dancing games once a week, and I was the worst in the class. Pauline was the best, though.'

'How about Posy?'

'Her mother was a dancer, she became a Fossil bringing ballet shoes with her, so I expect she'll be all right.' She fiddled with the gear lever. 'Do you suppose if you train to be a dancer and to act when you are eight like me, that you can be something else when you grow up?'

'Of course.' He laughed. 'Eight isn't very old. You've at least another ten years before you'll need to worry.'

'Oh, no.' Petrova shook her head. 'Nana says that Miss Dane says that we can start to earn money when we are twelve. I shall be twelve in four years. So if I begin earning then, I shall have been doing it for' – she counted on her fingers – 'five years by the time I'm quite grown up.'

'Meaning you'd be quite grown up at seventeen?'

'Yes. Well, would you think then I could be something else?'

'Of course. What do you want to be?'

'I don't know quite. Something to do with driving cars. Can girls be chauffeurs?'

'Lots are.'

She looked pleased.

'Then I think I'll be that.'

When they arrived at the Academy and rang the bell they were shown into a waiting-room. They had to wait in it quite a long time; but the children did not mind because of the pictures on the walls. These were photographs of the pupils of the school. Some were large ones of just one child. These were rather alike – the child wearing a ballet frock and standing on her toes. These were signed: 'To dear Madame Fidolia from Little Doris', or 'Babsy', or 'Baby Cora', or names like that. The children were most impressed by the way the children in the photographs stood on their points, but shocked at the signatures, considering them all too old to have names like 'Little' or 'Babsy' or 'Baby'.

They played a game giving marks for the handwritings; in the end a child signing herself 'Tiny' won. The photographs they liked better were the groups. These were of pantomimes, and though there were lots of Academy pupils in them, the children were not interested. What they liked were the other characters.

'Look,' said Posy, climbing on a seat to see better. 'That's *The Three Bears.*'

'It's not.' Pauline got up and joined her. 'It says it's *Puss in Boots.*'

Petrova came over to study the picture.

'I think it must have been called wrong. It is *The Three Bears.* What are those?'

Pauline put her head to one side hoping to see better.

'More like three cats, I think.'

'But there aren't three cats in *Puss in Boots,*' Posy objected. 'There's only one cat.'

Petrova suddenly gave an exclamation.

'Look. Those three cats aren't grown-up people; they are much smaller than that lady in tights.' She turned to Sylvia. 'Would you suppose when I'm twelve and can earn money I could be a cat? I wouldn't mind that.'

'No.' Pauline jumped off the bench. 'I'd love to be a cat, or a dog. A Pekingese would be nice to be – such a furry coat.'

'It's a monkey you'll be in a minute climbing about

messing yourself up,' Nana interrupted. 'Come and sit down like little ladies.'

Posy sat next to Sylvia.

'I'd rather be dressed like one of those little girls,' she said thoughtfully. 'I'd like to wear flowers in my hair.'

Pauline and Petrova looked at each other.

'Would you think,' said Pauline, 'that there could be so vain a child?' She turned to Posy. 'And I suppose you'd like to be called "Baby Posy"?'

'I wouldn't mind.' Posy swung her legs happily. 'I'd like to look like one of those children.'

Petrova leant over to her, and spoke in a very shocked voice.

'You wouldn't really like to look like one of those dressed-up misses? You wouldn't, Posy. You'd really much rather be a cat.'

'No.' Posy lolled against Sylvia. 'I'd like to wear flowers in my hair. Cats don't.'

'Very nice, too,' said Nana. 'Cats, indeed; it's the zoo you two ought to train at, not a dancing school.'

Pauline and Petrova both started to argue when they were interrupted. The door opened, and Madame Fidolia came in. Madame Fidolia had been a great dancer many years before; she had started training at the age of seven in the Russian Imperial Ballet School. She had made a big name for herself before the 1914 war, not only in Russia, but all over the world. When the revolution came she had to leave her country, for she had been a favourite with the Tsar and Tsarina, and so not popular with Soviet Russia. She made London her new home, and for some years danced there, as well as in most of the European capitals and America. Then one morning she had waked up and decided she was too old to dance any more. At the same time she realized she was too energetic a person to lead a lazy life, so she started her academy.

Madame Fidolia had thought, when she opened it, that she would run it as the Old Imperial Ballet School had been run. She soon found that was impossible, as it would cost far more money than pupils would pay. She found, too, that there were very few children who came to her who had real talent. She had discovered none of whom she had made a first-class ballerina. So she gave up trying to do the impossible, and ran an ordinary stage school where the children learnt all kinds of dancing, and actors came to teach them the art of acting. There was only one class through which they did not all pass, and that was Madame Fidolia's own. She watched every pupil who came through the school with care for about three to six months and then perhaps one day she would say: 'My child, you will come to my classes next term.' Going to Madame Fidolia's classes was the highest honour of the Academy.

The children thought her very odd-looking. She

had come straight from teaching. She had black hair parted in the middle and drawn down tight into a small bun on her neck. She had on a long practice-dress of white tarlatan, and pink tights, and pink ballet shoes. Round her shoulders she had a cerise silk shawl. She stood in the doorway.

'Miss Brown?' She had a very pretty, broken accent.

Sylvia got up.

'I'm Miss Brown.' They shook hands. Madame looked at the children.

'My pupils?'

'Yes. This is Pauline.'

Pauline smiled shyly and held out her hand, but Madame shook her head.

'No. All my children when they see me night and morning, and before and after a class, or any time when we meet say, "Madame" and curtsy. So!' She swept a lovely curtsy down to the floor.

Pauline turned scarlet, but she managed somehow, though it was more a bob than a curtsy, and only 'am' of 'Madame' could be heard.

'And this is Petrova.'

Petrova started her curtsy, but Madame came across to her. She took her face between her hands.

'Are you Russian?'

'Yes.'

'You speak Russian?' Madame's tone was full of hope.

'No.' Petrova looked anxiously at Sylvia, who came to her rescue explaining her history.

Madame kissed her.

'You are the first compatriot of mine to come to my school. I will make a good dancer of you. Yes?'

Petrova scratched at the floor with her toe and said nothing; she daren't look up, for she was sure Pauline would make her laugh.

'And this is Posy,' said Sylvia.

Posy came forward and dropped the most beautiful curtsy.

'Madame,' she said politely.

'Blessed lamb!' Nana murmured proudly.

'Little show-off!' Pauline whispered to Petrova.

Madame sent for Theo and told her to take them to the classroom, and they went into the junior dancing class. Here about twenty small girls in royal-blue rompers and white socks and black patent-leather shoes were learning tap-dancing. Theo spoke to the teacher. Madame, she said, wanted to see what classes to put these three children into. Madame sat down, and Sylvia and Nana sat beside her. The twenty little girls settled down cross-legged on the floor. Theo took the children to the middle of the room and told the pianist to play a simple polka, then she began to dance.

'You dance too, dears,' she said.

Pauline turned crimson. She had seen the sort of

31

thing the twenty children in the class were doing, and knew that she could do nothing like that, and that they were all younger than she was.

'Dance, Pauline, dear,' Theo called. 'Copy me.'

Pauline gave an agonized look at Sylvia, who smiled sympathy and encouragement, then she held out the skirts of her smock and began to polka.

Thank goodness we all know how to do this one, she thought. *We should have looked fools if it had been a waltz.*

Petrova began to polka straight away, but she did it very badly, stumbling over her feet.

'I won't mind,' she said to herself. 'I know I can't dance like all those children, so it's no good trying.'

She would not look at them, though, for she was sure they were whispering about her.

Posy was delighted to hear the music. Theo had taught her to polka, and she was charmed to show it off. She picked up her feet and held out her skirts, and pointed her toes; she thought it great fun.

'Just look at Posy!' Pauline whispered to Petrova as she passed her.

Petrova looked, and wished she could do it like that.

'Stop,' said Theo. 'Come here, dears.'

She took hold of the children one by one and lifted first their right legs and then their left over their heads. Then she left them and went to Madame Fidolia. She curtsied.

'Elementary, Madame?'

Madame got up; as she did so, all the children rose off the floor.

'Elementary,' she said. She shook first Sylvia and then Nana by the hand. 'Goodbye, children.'

She turned to go, and all the twenty children and the pianist and the instructress and Theo curtsied, saying 'Madame' in reverent voices. Pauline, Petrova, and Posy did it too, but a little late. Sylvia gave rather a deep bow, and Nana a bob.

'Well,' said Nana, as the door closed, 'if you ask me, it's for all the world like taking dancing classes in Buckingham Palace.'

'That's very satisfactory,' Theo explained to Sylvia. 'The elementary classes are from four to five every afternoon. The acting classes are on Saturdays, so that all the children can be brought together. It will be more difficult later on, when they are in different classes.'

They went home on a bus.

'Do you know,' Pauline whispered to Petrova as they sat down together on the front seat on the top, 'that soon it's Posy's birthday, when we have to do our vows again, and we can't.'

'Why not?'

'Well, didn't we vow to make Fossil a name in history books? Whoever heard of people on the stage in history books?'

'We needn't be actresses always, though,' Petrova said comfortingly. 'I asked Mr Simpson, and he said because you were a thing from the time you were twelve till you grew up it didn't mean you had to be it always.'

'It's difficult to see how to be in a history book, anyway,' Pauline said, in a worried sort of voice. 'It's mostly Kings and Queens who are. People like Princess Elizabeth will be; but not us whatever we did – at least, it will be difficult.'

'There's Joan of Arc.' Petrova tried to remember a few more names. 'I know there were a lot, but I didn't get as far as a whole reign, I was only doing *Tales from History* when we left Cromwell House. Then I did that little bit about Alfred the Great with Garnie; and Doctor Jakes hasn't given me a history lesson yet. But there were lots. I know there were. We'll ask Doctor Jakes to tell us about them.'

Sylvia leant over from the seat behind.

'Look, darlings, here is a shilling. I want you all to have cakes for tea to make up for a very hard-working afternoon.'

The Fossils became some of the busiest children in London. They got up at half-past seven and had breakfast at eight. After breakfast they did exercises with Theo for half an hour. At nine they began lessons. Posy did two hours' reading, writing, and

kindergarten work with Sylvia, and Pauline and
Petrova did three hours with Doctor Jakes and Doctor
Smith. They were very interesting lessons, but terribly
hard work; for if Doctor Smith was teaching Pauline,
Doctor Jakes taught Petrova, and the other way on,
and as both doctors had spent their lives coaching
people for terribly stiff examinations – though of
course they taught quite easy things to the children –
they never got the idea out of their minds that a stiff
examination was a thing everybody had to pass some
day. There was a little break of ten minutes in the
middle of the morning when milk and biscuits were
brought in; but after a day or two they were never
eaten or drunk. Both doctors had lovely ideas about
the sort of things to have in the middle of lessons – a
meal they called a beaver. They took turns to get it
ready. Sometimes it was chocolate with cream on it,
and sometimes Doctor Jakes's ginger drink, and once it
was ice-cream soda; and the things to eat were never
the same: queer biscuits, little ones from Japan with
delicate flowers painted on them in sugar, cakes from
Vienna, and specialities of different kinds from all
over England. They had their beavers sitting round
the fire in either of the doctors' rooms, and they had
discussions which were nothing to do with lessons. At
twelve o'clock they went for a walk with Nana or
Sylvia. They liked it best when Sylvia took them. She
had better ideas about walks; she thought the Park the

place to go to, and thought it a good idea to take hoops and things to play with. Nana liked a nice clean walk up as far as the Victoria and Albert and back. On wet days Sylvia thought it a good plan to stay in and make toffee or be read out loud to. Nana thought nicely brought-up children ought to be out of the house between twelve and one, even on a wet day, and she took them to see the dolls' houses in the Victoria and Albert. The children liked the dolls' houses; but there are a lot of wet days in the winter, and they saw them a good deal. Pauline and Petrova had lunch with Sylvia, Posy had hers with Nana. After lunch they all had to take a book on their beds for half an hour. In the afternoons there was another walk, this one always with Nana. It lasted an hour, and as they had usually walked to the Victoria and Albert in the morning, they did not have to go there again, but took turns to choose where they went. Pauline liked walking where there were shops. Petrova liked the Earl's Court Road, because there were three motor showrooms for her to look at. Posy liked to go towards the King's Road, Chelsea, because on the way they passed a shop that sold puppies. They all liked Posy's walk; but they did not choose it them- selves because they knew she would. If Nana was not so sure that they must save the penny and walk they would have gone to much more exciting places; for you can't get far on your legs when there is only an hour, and that includes getting home again. Tea was in the nursery at a quarter to four, and at half past they went by the Piccadilly railway to Russell Square. They all liked going on the underground; but both Gloucester Road, where they got in, and Russell Square, where they got out, were those mean sort of stations that have lifts instead of moving staircases.

'Going to dancing class,' Petrova said almost every day, 'wouldn't be so bad if only there was even one moving staircase.'

As soon as they got to the Academy they went down to the changing-room. There they shared a locker in which lived their rompers and practice-frocks and shoes. Their rompers were royal blue with C.A. for Children's Academy embroidered on the pockets. They wore their rompers for the first half-hour, and with them white socks and black patent-leather ankle-strapped shoes. In these clothes they did exercises and a little dancing which was known as 'character', also twice a week they worked at tap-dancing. At the end of half an hour they hung towels round their necks (for they were supposed to get so hot they would need a wipe down) and went back to the changing-room and put on their white tarlatan practice-frocks. These were like overalls with no join down the back; the bodice had hooks and the frills of the skirt wrapped over and clipped. With this they wore white socks and white kid slippers. The work they did in these dresses they found dull, and it made their legs ache. They did not realize that the half-hour spent holding on to a bar and doing what they thought stupid exercises was very early training for ballet. Ballet to them meant wearing blocked shoes like the little pair that had come with Posy or such as the more advanced classes wore at school. Sometimes Madame Fidolia came in to watch their class, and directly she arrived they all let go of the practice-bar and curtsied to the floor saying 'Madame'.

They got home at half-past six, and Posy went straight to bed. Sylvia read to the other two for twenty minutes, and then Petrova had to go up, and at seven, Pauline. The lights were out by half past and there was no more talking.

On Saturday mornings they worked from ten to one at the Academy. As well as special exercise classes and the ordinary dancing classes, there was singing, and one hour's acting class. For these they wore the Academy overalls. They were of black sateen made from a Russian design, with high collars, and double-breasted, buttoning with large black buttons down the left side; round the waist they had wide black leather belts. With these they wore their white sandals.

Petrova, who hated clothes, found the everlasting changing an awful bore. Saturdays were the worst.

'Oh, I do hate Saturdays,' she said to Nana. 'I get

up in my jersey and skirt, and as soon as I get to the Academy I change everything, even put a vest on instead of my combinations, and wear those rompers; and then my practice-dress and then the overall; and then back into my combinations and my skirt and jersey. I wish I was a savage who wore nothing.'

'That's no way to talk,' Nana told her severely. 'Many a poor little child would be glad of the nice clothes you wear; and as for changing out of your combies, I'm glad you do; you wear holes in them fast enough without all that dancing in them.'

From the very beginning Madame took an interest in Posy. Each class that she came to watch she made her do some step alone. Posy had her shoes taken off one day and her instep looked at; Madame was so delighted at the shape and flexibility of her feet that she called the rest of the class to look at them. The rest of the class admired them while Madame was there, but secretly none of them could see anything about them different from their own. Pauline and Petrova thought it very bad for Posy to be made so conspicuous, and to teach her not to get cocky they called her 'Posy-Pretty-Toes' all the way home. Posy hated it, and at last burst into tears. Nana was very cross.

'That's right, you two, tease poor little Posy; she can't help Madame saying she has nice feet. It's jealous, that's what you are. Any more of your nonsense and you'll go to bed half an hour early.'

39

'Why should we be jealous?' asked Petrova. 'Who cares what feet look like? They are just useful things.'

Pauline giggled.

'Have you pretty feet, Nana?' She looked down at Nana's square-toed black shoes which she always wore.

'I have what God gave me,' Nana said reverently, 'and they're all I need, never having thoughts to dance in a ballet.'

The thought of Nana, who was very fat, dancing in a ballet made them all laugh so much that they forgot to call Posy 'Pretty-Toes' again, and they were still laughing when they got home.

It was at the acting classes that Pauline shone. The acting in their first term was entirely in mime. They acted whole fairy stories without saying a word. Whether she was a princess, or a peasant, or an old man, Pauline managed to make them real without any dressing up, but just in the way she moved.

At singing classes none of them shone. They could keep in tune, but that was all – they were in no way distinguished.

Just before Christmas the school broke up for a month. All the senior girls were working in panto-mimes, and for some time all those who were not old enough for licences had felt very unimportant. The children's classes were moved from one room to another to make room for rehearsals, and the notice-board was covered with rehearsal calls. 'All concerned in the Rose Ballet, in room three at 4.30.' 'The children appearing in *Red Riding Hood*, 5.30, room seven.' 'The principals for the Jewel Ballet, 4 o'clock, room one.' And, as well, calls for the children stars. 'Poppy: 10.30 with Madame Fidolia.' 'Winifred: 12 o'clock with Madame Fidolia.'

Pauline, Petrova, and Posy would gaze in great awe at these names.

'Winifred,' one of them would say – 'that's the girl who wears a fur coat. Poppy is going to be Alice in Wonderland. She's the one with the long hair.'

They would peep through the glass on the doors of the rooms where the rehearsals were taking place, and stare at the children who were already twelve and old enough to earn money.

'Not this Christmas, but the one after I shall be one of those children,' Pauline said enviously.

Marcia
Knowles

Sally Cinderella

BERNARD ASHLEY

Coming up to date for a while, and in a complete story this time, we move away from the hard-up middle classes of the thirties and come to south London's multi-ethnic Clipper Street, where hands from the school reach out into the shops and the homes around.

Sally never seemed right, never looked up to very much. Some people have the knack of looking good all the time – every day Queen of the May. They might be dressed in old clothes and climbing out of a pigsty but they somehow sparkle and smile, their eyes come through, and you can always take a photo you'd like to keep. Handsome. Pretty. Really up to the mark.

But others could spend a year in front of a mirror

and they still wouldn't get a stare from a cat. Perhaps it all comes from inside: and there are some people who feel so miserable most of the time they don't care whether they're walking to a party – or off the nearest bridge. And Sally Lane knew more about pavements than she did about the sky, knew tree roots better than the leaves. A smile for her would have worked muscles that hurt. It wasn't the same for her sisters – it wasn't the same for the dog – but that's how it was for Sally.

She was up and dressed and down at the shop before most of the others had opened their eyes.

'Fags,' her mother said one morning, 'an' sugar.' She gave her no money, just pressed her pencil message into a soft piece of cardboard: soft-looking words, hard heart, because her mother knew that certain stupid people felt sorry for Sally Lane. She was always the one to send when she wasn't going to pay.

Mrs Vasisht was one of them: and so was Kompel, who helped in the shop when she wasn't at school. Sally was only six but everyone seemed to know her.

'Yeah?' Kompel asked as the thin little girl slid in round the door.

Sally gave up the note, her eyes as usual on the floor. Kompel took it gently – because a quick-moving arm would make her flinch, she knew.

'Hang on. I'll have to ask.'

Sally waited. She was used to this. Not paying

usually meant a bit of fuss. She yawned, eyed the fresh bread, smelt its heat.

'Sorry, tell your mother no cigarettes.' Mrs Vasisht had come out. 'Sugar OK, but no cigarettes.' She waved her fingers in a 'no' sign. 'Cigarettes only for grown-ups. Little children not allowed.' The shop-keeper's face was unsmiling, but then she was unsmiling with everyone, she wasn't picking on Sally.

Kompel gave Sally the smallest packet of sugar on the shelf. 'It's the law, Sal,' she explained. 'See? My mum and dad gets into trouble if they sell cigarettes to kids . . .'

Sally stared at her, took back the cardboard note with *cigarettes* crossed through, walked out of the shop. She sighed as she went and her steps were slower than they had been coming. Slower steps, faster heart – because going home without the full message meant she'd done wrong. And doing wrong always got her a good hiding.

Kompel may have been hard worked, but she had never been hard hit. Working hard in the shop was natural, was expected. You didn't sit and watch much telly when your dad was stuck behind a post-office grille all day and only came out on short visits; when your mum kept the shop doors open all the time there was light in the sky. Everyone in the family worked. Even little Sunil had to carry cola bottles and jump his frail weight on cardboard boxes.

But no one ever got hit. Dad might hold your hand hard, or look at you that sad way. But hard hitting was for ants, and beetles, and mice. And the only other sort was for backs, soft pats, when people were pleased with you.

Kompel worked hard in school, too. She was good at maths because maths was what she *had* to know. Weights and litres and money – checking the red numbers on the till with her brain for homework, getting the change correct. And that helped to make school a good place to go. To get things right, to draw and dance and write poetry: all of which came from inside, from the energy of the sun that seemed to shine within her.

On the morning of the cigarettes Kompel got to the playground just before the bell, didn't have time for a game with anyone. But she did see Sally Lane, standing on her own over by the kitchen – watching her sisters playing chase.

Kompel shrugged. *No cigarettes* wasn't down to her, was it? She couldn't make everything right for Sally. And she definitely couldn't make Sally's sisters play with her.

The bell was just about to go – and so was Kompel, when Sally stared over at her and suddenly twisted herself away again. A sort of, *You!* look. *You!*

Well, it wasn't my fault! Kompel told herself. I'm sorry – but I didn't make the law about selling

46

cigarettes. All the same, it had annoyed her, little Sally's huff. She felt *sorry* for her, she didn't deserve that sort of a look.

The first bell went, and most people stopped. Then the second, and they started going in. The runners who thought they couldn't be seen, the walkers who hoped they could, and the have-another-kick boys who didn't care one way or the other.

Sally, being good, pulled herself off her wall and came towards Kompel. And Kompel, a monitor and expected in last, stood there and stared at her.

What was that? Sally looked different somehow, even to this morning. She wasn't the same as when she'd come into the shop before school. Not quite. Something was different about her. Around the face.

Her cheek was swollen. She'd got a red, fiery mark under her eye, and she'd been crying.

'Wassup, Sal? What you done?'

But Sally barely gave Kompel the time for an answer. She hurried on past, her eyes on the grey of the ground. 'Door swang back,' she said.

And that was all. No being cross with it, the way people are.

And definitely no details.

Kompel had another good day. She was in on a few laughs, wrote a long piece about the month of May, won at volley-ball. She should have gone home happy.

But somehow she didn't, couldn't – and Sally Lane was the cause of that. Her bad face had stayed with Kompel all day.

Poor little kid, she thought, being sent to school with a hurting face. No ointment on it. No plaster. Not seen to, probably, because they were cross with her over going home without the fags. By playtime one of the Helpers had put cream on it, but that wasn't the same as having her mum or her dad look after her, was it?

Kompel got home and turned to in the shop. They were always busy with kids after school, tons of them, buying penny chews and picture-cards. You needed eyes everywhere: more like being a teacher than a shopkeeper. But, as her mum said, don't look down your nose at it. It was all the cheap bits, the small packets, which kept the corner shop going. They all went to Asda for their big stuff; and came here for what was handy. And for the slate, when they wanted tick.

The 'slate' was the book where Kompel's mother wrote what people owed. People with regular business at the post-office counter could run up little bills – then on paying-out day they had to settle.

And being Thursday, Mrs Lane came in for the post office, after the main rush.

No one could tell how hard she was on Sally, not by looking at her. She seemed an ordinary sort of person, not some cruel witch. She'd got little Lindy with her, and she bought her a Twix, stroking the kid's white-blonde hair, settling up her bill like Lady Muck.

'Sorry about cigarettes,' Kompel's mother said to her. 'We're having to be very careful right now.'

'Oh, that's all right, love. Just can't start the day without a fag, can I, Lind?'

Lindy shook her head as if it were a known fact, like those you learned in school. Important.

'Fag an' a cough get me going.'

If you asked her, Kompel couldn't tell what made her say what she did. All she knew was that she suddenly heard herself saying it – with a somersault in her stomach to tell her she was really taking a chance.

'Shame about Sally's face,' she said.

Mrs Lane turned and stared at her, cold. It was like looking into the face of some dangerous animal which might suddenly spring, and bite you.

'Yeah!' she said. 'Clumsy little cat, weren't she, Lind? Fell down the steps.'

Lindy nodded: didn't bat an eye.

Mrs Lane's voice was flat and freezing. Lindy's eyes were like ice. But the real chill was in Kompel's stomach.

Falling down the steps wasn't what Sally had said. '*Door swang back,*' had been her words. Different stories. And neither of them was the truth, Kompel guessed. Because to be honest with herself, she'd known all day, hadn't she? Little Sally Lane hadn't had an accident. She'd been punched, like an enemy.

'You don't get involved in all that,' Kompel's mother told her late that night. And her father made that clicking noise in his throat which said he agreed with her. 'It's bad business to tell tales on customers. People soon stop coming in if they think we're secret police.'

Three sentences, quickly spoken: but adding up to a terrible moment for Kompel. One she'd probably remember all her life. She'd remember the meal they'd just had and where all the things were on the table. Because it was the first time that she knew her parents were in the wrong, putting the family in front of what was right.

'How do you think it looks, eh, if an Indian family reports on them for cruelty, for this child abuse? How long before a brick comes through that window?' Her father's eyes seemed bigger than ever, his own skin more pale from the long days in his post-office cell.

'An' how do you think it feels to have a punch in the face – and no one cares?' Kompel had never answered him back before. 'She's a little kid – she's six!'

'The school will know. They don't shut their eyes to things like that.'

'Not like you do, you mean!' Kompel got up and

ran to her room. Angry. Crying. But leaving a long silence behind her which said they knew she was right.

The bruise on Sally's face got better, and quite quickly – almost as if the stares which Kompel gave her were some sort of ointment. And looking, smiling, saying something nice was all Kompel could do not to feel helpless.

She would have liked to do more, but there wasn't really the chance. She would have liked to make sure Sally never went home without her full message, for a start. She would have liked to talk to Sally about that bruise, if ever she could find a way: just to let her know that someone cared. And to talk about the rest of it all. Kompel had never seen anyone who looked so unhappy all the time, in among a family of kids who laughed and played and looked all right. Out at play in Clipper Street, up at the top end where the cars couldn't go, they'd all be there with the others. But Sally would be talking to a wall or crouching to an ant, out of it, silent, while the rest made more noise than a treeful of starlings.

'Here, what's up with Sally?' Kompel asked her little brother Bobby, who was still fat with paddi-pants and too young not to talk. 'She a naughty girl indoors?'

'Naughty!' He nodded his head fiercely. 'Won't go

a-sleep. Nick the biscuits.' His little face was overtaken with the horror of it, and the hatred.

'Oh.' Kompel pretended to understand. Then, in a low voice so that his sisters wouldn't hear, 'Gets smacks, does she?'

Little Bobby looked at her: his lips went all stiff with the seriousness of Sally having to be smacked all the time for being so naughty. And he suddenly turned and toddled away – as if the family silence about smacks was something he'd just that second understood.

From now on Kompel had an aim in life. To make Sally Lane smile. It wasn't a great aim, not a changing-the-world sort of thing, not even a medium aim like changing Sally's family for a nicer one. But just this small aim of changing the look on Sally's face for a second or two.

She gave the girl sweets. She found a packet of picture-cards with the wrapper torn and took them to school for her. She tried to get her into a game. But it was somehow as if Sally suspected that Kompel was trying to unlock her secret – as if she was scared of something worse which might happen if she did. And she wouldn't give an inch: not a millimetre of a smile. She took what was given to her and went back inside herself, staring at the lower half of the world with eyes which never shone.

In the classroom, though, where Kompel didn't see her, Sally played a clever game. She behaved more like the rest: she answered a few questions, read her reading book, played with the dolls when she got the chance. (And smacked them a lot for being naughty.) She was like someone who didn't want to stand out – except still she never smiled.

Kompel got nowhere near her aim. And, what was worse, one morning she really let Sally down. Right in the middle of her get-a-smile campaign, Kompel did the unforgivable. She switched off her alarm and turned over in bed. And was cross with herself when she found out from her mother that Sally had been into the shop.

'Mrs Lane, she skipped out pretty quick yesterday. Didn't settle up. And this morning she sends for a list as long as you like. No money again! All on the slate!'

'Who came?'

'That one. Little Sally.'

'What did you do?' If ever Kompel had needed to be there to make it all right!

'I gave her cornflakes and milk for the breakfast. For the children. But I told her, send her mother in to see me for the rest.'

Kompel kept her mouth shut tight, didn't make a row again. After all, what else would she have been able to do that was better? Just made sure the cigarettes were in, for Mrs Lane's morning cough? Yes! She'd definitely have done that, if she'd been about. That would have helped. And it was a warm summer morning, no need to have turned over in bed . . .

It went on to be a very hot day: like being on the equator. The first really hot day of the year in school and it was cotton dresses on, T-shirts off and pushing for drinks at the water taps. The cooks came in moaning about the heat as if they'd been putting up with it for weeks. And Mr Ransom drove his car in slowly with the top down . . .

In all of which Sally Lane wore a long-sleeved woolly cardigan. The rest of London was fanning itself in the hot still air and Sally Lane was dressed for the cold.

'You all right, Sal?' Kompel looked hard at the girl's face. But Sally's eyes said she couldn't trust her kindness: she couldn't afford to let anyone feel sorry for her. She stared back at Kompel, and walked on away.

'I only asked!' Kompel exploded. And then felt sorry. Didn't Sally get enough of the rough end of tongues?

It was one of those days that could have been bad tempered all round. In assembly all the windows had to be open and London came roaring in. The push, push, push of the traffic, the throaty drone of the low-level aircraft coming in to land at Heathrow. It was too hot to sing very well, and the announcements were given in the gaps between the heavy lorries. It would have been in and straight out except for one thing. Infants' May Day, coming up the week before half-term: dancing round the maypole and crowning the Queen of the May. And today the names came out of the hat. The May Queen and the May Prince, chosen by chance from the Infants' top class.

Mrs Peters was there with the two cardboard boxes (no one had a hat). A big 'Q' marked the Queen box, a big 'P' the Prince: and not a hint of pink or blue.

The Juniors were hot and bored, but this was a big moment for the thirty top Infants, and everyone was shushed to sit ready to clap the lucky two. Kompel remembered. It would be a big day for them when it came. The procession, the crowning, the local paper with the big camera and all the parents with theirs. A day of being special, of fame. She hadn't had it herself, but she could remember the thrill of it for Wendy Dorsett, whose smile hadn't faded for a week.

'So who are the two going to be?' Mrs Peters was asking. 'Well, today we're going to find out!'

Twenty-nine straight backs, twenty-nine bright faces with tight smiles. And Sally Lane, hunched in her cardigan, sucking her thumb.

Everyone waited.

'And in Clipper Primary School tradition we'll ask two Year Six leavers to pull out the names. A big boy and a big girl,' she explained for the Infants. 'Let's see now . . .' Mrs Peters squinted to the back of the hall for a couple of good faces. 'John Lunn . . . and . . . Kompel Vasisht.'

With heavy sighs of responsibility John and Kompel pulled themselves up and stepped over to the front. And even something like that got your heart beating, Kompel found, even in your own school. All the eyes! But in a couple of minutes she was going to find her heart beating a lot harder still . . .

John Lunn was efficiency itself. When your father was a river-pilot and your mother was a teacher you didn't need too much telling how to do such things. In went his hand and out came, 'Sullaiman Shamime' – said very confidently.

'Thank you, John.'

Two hundred heads craned and twisted to find Sullaiman – who was the one Infant suddenly interested in the velcro on his trainers.

'So Sullaiman's our May Prince this year. And . . .' Mrs Peters smiled all round, and she nodded at Kompel. The hall was very hot now. *Let's get this over and get out*, she seemed to be saying, one old hand to another.

Kompel's fingers dipped into the box Mrs Peters was holding above her. And it was then, in a sudden pound, that her heart knew what her head was going to do. And her head went all swimmy as she did it: as she tried to make everything up to Sally Lane: to bring the ghost of a smile to her sad face, just for a second. As Kompel's hand came out of the box she saw her, the hunched-over kid who thought she was no part of anything like this.

Marcia Knowles was the name written on the paper in beautiful italic. And *Sally Lane* was the name Kompel read out – with hardly a falter, nearly as well as John Lunn had done.

It was as if she'd pressed a small button: a faint-sounding buzzer going there in the hall. Teachers looked at one another and said things with their eyes. The other Lane children looked as if they'd drunk medicine. Someone coughed.

And Mrs Peters, in that electric moment, asked to see the piece of paper. 'May I?' she said, in the voice she used when she was checking work you'd marked yourself.

Looking away, Kompel gave the paper to her. She had to give it, there was no alternative – she was like a prisoner who had to stand up straight in court while the damning evidence was read. She'd been so stupid! Why had she let herself get carried away? She had always been trusted, the teachers liked her, and the little kids thought she was grown up, what with the shop and everything. And now she was going to look like the biggest cheat going.

Mrs Peters read the name on the paper to herself. She stared at Kompel. And she straight away said, 'Thank you, Kompel. And well done, Sally, you'll make a good May Queen.' She screwed the paper into her pocket and started the clapping – a movement of the air in the hall coming just soon enough to stop Kompel from fainting.

And still Sally didn't smile. She just stared up at Kompel and sucked harder on her thumb.

There was no inquest over it. No more was said. Perhaps Mrs Peters didn't know how to deal with such a thing – Kompel showing everyone how she felt about little Sally. One thing was certain: Kompel was sure the teachers never knew. No one ever looked at her any differently for pulling that name from the hat. But whatever Mrs Peters did or didn't do, Kompel wouldn't have known anyway, because that went on in the private way things do in the staff-room.

Each class teacher was organizing their own different dance for the day. Mrs Gullivar was seeing to the Prince and his crown and robes. And Mrs MacKay, the deputy head, was in charge of the costume for the Queen – the dress for Sally to wear.

'I'll see how it fits,' she said. Every year there were alterations to be made. The crown never needed to fit any better than the real Queen's, crowns just need careful balancing, but the dress had to be up to the mark.

Mrs Walker pulled a snobby face. 'Ugh! I don't know how you can bear to touch that child!' She drove in from Kent each day to teach at Clipper Primary. 'I'd be washing my hands for a week!'

Mrs MacKay half ignored her. 'Oh, she's not so bad, poor little devil,' she said, whisking the dress out of the staff-room smoke; only her blotchy neck showing her anger.

Sally Lane had been kept behind in her classroom. Sullaiman Shamime was finished and gone, his Prince's robes hanging up like a giant puppet.

'Now then, let's see . . .' Mrs MacKay said. She held the shiny pink dress up to Sally. 'Stand up straight, love.'

Sally looked at her warily, some great fear behind her eyes.

'Looks all right for length. Perhaps we'll turn the hem just half an inch.' The hem went up and down regularly, had as many needle holes as it had material. 'Now, do we need a tuck in the back?' Mrs MacKay could have been talking to some forlorn little statue. 'I hope you'll give us a May Queen's smile on the day, eh? Mummy *will* be pleased.' But it was just words. They both knew the game that was being played – pretend, pretend, pretend. 'Now, cardy off – we shan't have that on, on the day . . .'

But now the statue moved. Sally drew back, re-sisted, and spoke. 'Mustn't,' she said. 'My mum told me.' She was gripping the bottoms of the cardigan arms with her small, chewed fingers. 'I got a cold.'

'Oh, come on. It's a lovely hot day. I'll take the blame!' And like the firm mother she was herself, Mrs MacKay had the cardigan off. 'One, two, three!'

While *four* and all the way to twenty was silent at the sight of Sally's arm — where a bite, a red and white human bite, told its own terrible story.

'How did this happen?' Mrs Peters asked her kindly, in her room. 'Who did this to you?'

Sally Lane stared sullenly at the floor.

'Eh?' the headteacher asked, as if Sally had answered and she just hadn't heard. 'Sally — how did this happen?' She waited, patiently, with just the raising of her eyebrows.

There was a long, long wait.

'Come on!' she said, just a bit more sharply.

'King,' Sally murmured. 'Our dog.'

'Oh, King! But his mouth's not this shape, is it? A dog's mouth is different altogether. Lovie, I can see the tooth marks . . .

'Didn't anyone treat it?' Mrs MacKay asked. 'No Savlon?' She dropped her voice. 'And what about your bad face the other day?'

But Sally was back to staring. They knew. Her

eyes, suddenly sharp, said it all. The game was up –
her mum's and dad's game – but she didn't want to
get worse done to her for saying . . .

'This is a . . . person's . . . bite, Sally. And a big
person's. Now, who was it? We've got to know,
you'll have to tell someone . . .'

No amount of cajoling or explaining got another
word out of her, though. No amount of being made
to feel safe. No amount of telling how the school *had*
to ring Social Services, and how Social Services *had* to
look into it. Sally clammed right up, as if being
forgiven for not telling was the last little thread of
hope she had to hold on to.

The woman from Social Services was very kind – Ms
Partridge, to be called Penny. She came quickly and
she took Sally home to her parents. She showed them
Sally's bad arm; and, very quietly, she wanted to
know how it had happened.

The children were sent to play out at the back, and
in a calm, friendly, firm way she let them know what
the score was. What her powers were. How her office
knew where she was and how they needn't bother
shouting or abusing or threatening. All they had to do
was tell her.

She made it clear that Sally herself had said nothing,
except to blame the dog: but that no one had believed
that, and they certainly wouldn't when a doctor took

a look at that arm. She also set the school's part of it straight: they hadn't poked or pried, it was all over the May Queen, as simple as that.

'May Queen!' Brian Lane suddenly broke his fierce silence. 'Ain't they s'posed to *teach* 'em? May Queen!' He looked as if he had a lot more shout in him, too, but his wife gave him a look and he shut up. Left his leg dangling over the armchair to show whose house it was.

Very matter of fact, puffing smoke, Sally's mother went through different stories of the bite. The dog, it *must* have been: Sally often annoyed him, which is why she hadn't shown them her bad arm. Or if it was human it had to be a big kid at school: there was a lot had it in for Sally. And how did they know it wasn't a teacher? God, some of the teachers *she'd* had as a kid! Half killed you and nothing got said.

But Ms Partridge had an answer to everything. The shape of the bite. The size of the different tooth marks. How a doctor and a dentist could match it with the mouth that did it – and would, if need be. She ran the Lanes into dead-ends, to places their stories couldn't go – till anger and frustration suddenly had Brian Lane bursting out with the truth.

'All right! I done it!' he shouted. 'Clever-puss, ain't you? You don't know her, the little madam! She's trouble from the minute she wakes up to the minute she goes to bed!'

'Gave me a bad time from the off,' his wife said, patting her stomach as if Sally had committed some crime in the womb. 'Could be her middle name, Trouble. Never stopped crying, gave us a hell of a time, broken nights . . .'

'She gets fed proper, gets dressed nice. Then it's always after more – want, want, want. Lies. Steals. You need a lock on that fridge. Took the dog's dinner once . . .'

'A right little cat. There's no pleasing her . . .'

Ms Partridge kept her eyes down and took some notes, matter of fact.

But she wasn't the only one listening. Sally was outside the door, listening to her parents listing their love for her. And her eyes glazed over, as if even the painful bite couldn't hurt hard enough to keep her sharp. As if nothing could hurt very much against the Council being told all this . . .

Kompel never knew quite what happened. Some true stories aren't wrapped up in endings for everyone taking part in them to read. She'd never actually known about the arm: not even all the teachers had known about that. And she didn't know about Social Services, nor how the school had only been waiting to jump on to something certain before calling them in.

But she did see something of the change she'd made

by reading that false name from the hat, although she never knew it had anything to do with her.

All at once there were new dresses for everyone to see. And Sally walking with her sisters – and not being the one who did all the messages while the rest of them laid in bed.

And she was the May Queen, with her mother coming to clap her, all on her best behaviour. Sally Lane did that ever so well, Kompel thought – went through all the right moves and remembered where to stand. Almost smiled when a footballer put the crown on her head; was very special for a day.

But Kompel never knew who helped to make sure it happened. Further up Clipper Street, though, some of the neighbours knew Ms Partridge and what she did. They saw the regular car outside, noticed how the shouting from the Lanes' house got quieter, except when it was, 'Sally, *love*,' all very loud and clear.

And from behind their net curtains some of them knew about the deals Social Services did with people like the Lanes. *We'll help you, but only if you try.* We're keeping a good eye on you, and one step out of line, one more bruise or burn or bite or stripe and we'll throw the book at you – and see the mark *that* makes!

They knew Sally understood. How she was on a deal, too. A deal to tell. There were to be no more dark secrets, not any more. She even had a number to ring.

And all at once, she had the power. She could get what she wanted some days with no more than a hard stare at the others. Things like biscuits, and sweets, and she even got to see what she wanted on the television. Well, the neighbours said, after what she'd been through, didn't she deserve it?

But there wasn't any deal on love. Social Services couldn't quite make that happen.

Kompel worked on in the shop and she saw Sally Lane come in and go out, growing up, looking more and more people in the eye every day: even got given a hard look herself when she didn't get round to serving the girl fast enough. And once she heard Sally swearing at her father behind his post-office grille. But she pretended not to see, not to hear. How could the girl know what was normal?

Kompel never regretted what she'd done that day in assembly. And she would always be grateful to Mrs Peters for making it her secret, too. Because didn't you have to help Cinderellas like Sally? Make allowances for them?

And just hope that one day they might get the chance to start living happily ever after . . .

The Mile

GEORGE LAYTON

I used to sit next to an older boy who pinched with his nails and who would hit me in the playground if I ever shouted loud enough to get him into trouble. I can also remember my day-dreams of doing a Saint George and rescuing Wendy Kemp from some terrible fate about to befall her, to her everlasting gratitude: so reading *The Mile* is almost as if George Layton had written this story for me, as our experiences of growing up seem to have been so similar, him in the north and me in the south.

What a rotten report. It was the worst report I'd ever had. I'd dreaded bringing it home for my mum to read. We were sitting at the kitchen table having our tea, but neither of us had touched anything. It was gammon and chips as well, with a pineapple ring. My favourite. We have gammon every Friday, cos my Auntie Doreen works on the bacon counter at the Co-op, and she drops it in on her way home. I don't think she pays for it.

My mum was reading the report for the third time. She put it down on the table and stared at me. I didn't say anything. I just stared at my gammon and chips and pineapple ring. What could I say? My mum looked so disappointed. I really felt sorry for her. She was determined for me to do well at school, and get my O levels, then get my A levels, then go to university, then get my degree, and then get a good job with good prospects . . .

'I'm sorry, Mum . . .'

She picked up the report again, and started reading it for the fourth time.

'It's no good reading it again, Mum. It's not going to get any better.'

She slammed the report back on to the table.

'Don't you make cheeky remarks to me. I'm not in the mood for it!'

I hadn't meant it to be cheeky, but I suppose it came out like that.

'I wouldn't say anything if I was you, after reading this report!'

I shrugged my shoulders.

'There's nothing much I *can* say, is there?'

'You can tell me what went wrong. You told me you worked hard this term!'

I *had* told her I'd worked hard, but I hadn't.

'I did work hard, Mum.'

'Not according to this.'

She waved the report under my nose.

'You're supposed to be taking your O levels next year. What do you think is going to happen then?'

I shrugged my shoulders again, and stared at my gammon and chips.

'I don't know.'

She put the report back on the table. I knew I hadn't done well in my exams cos of everything that had happened this term, but I didn't think for one moment I'd come bottom in nearly everything. Even Norbert Lightowler had done better than me.

'You've come bottom in nearly everything. Listen to this.'

She picked up the report again.

'Maths – inattentive and lazy.'

I knew what it said.

'I know what it says, Mum.'

She leaned across the table, and put her face close to mine.

'I know what it says too, and I don't like it.'

She didn't have to keep reading it.

'Well, stop reading it then.'

My mum just gave me a look.

'English Language – he is capricious and dilettante. What does that mean?'

I turned the pineapple ring over with my fork. Oh heck, was she going to go through every rotten subject?

'Come on – English Language – Mr Melrose says you're "capricious and dilettante". What does he mean?'

'I don't know!'

I hate Melrose. He's really sarcastic. He loves making a fool of you in front of other people. Well, he could stick his 'capricious and dilettante', and his rotten English Language, and his set books, and his horrible breath that nearly knocks you out when he stands over you.

'I don't know what he means.'

'Well, you should know. That's why you study English Language, to understand words like that. It means you mess about, and don't frame yourself.'

My mum kept reading every part of the report over and over again. It was all so pointless. It wasn't as if reading it over and over again was going to change anything. Mind you, I kept my mouth shut. I just sat there staring at my tea. I knew her when she was in this mood.

'What I can't understand is how come you did so well at Religious Instruction? You got seventy-five per cent.'

I couldn't understand that either.

'I like Bible stories, Mum.' She wasn't sure if I was cheeking her or not. I wasn't.

'Bible stories? It's all I can do to get you to come to St Cuthbert's one Sunday a month with me and your Auntie Doreen.'

That was true, but what my mum didn't know was that the only reason I went was cos my Auntie Doreen slips me a few bob!

'And the only reason you go then is cos your Auntie Doreen gives you pocket money.'

'Aw, that's not true, Mum.'

Blimey! My mum's got eyes everywhere.

She put the report back into the envelope. Hurray! The Spanish Inquisition was over. She took it out again. Trust me to speak too soon.

'I mean, you didn't even do well at sport, did you? "Sport – he is not a natural athlete." Didn't you do *anything* right this term?'

I couldn't help smiling to myself. No, I'm not a natural athlete, but I'd done one thing right this term. I'd shown Arthur Boocock that he couldn't push me around any more. That's why everything else had gone wrong. That's why I was 'lazy and inattentive' at Maths, and 'capricious and dilettante' at English Language. That's why this last term had been so miserable, cos of Arthur blooming Boocock.

He'd only come into our class this year because

he'd been kept down. I didn't like him. He's a right bully, but because he's a bit older and is good at sport and running and things, everybody does what he says.

That's how Smokers' Corner started.

Arthur used to pinch his dad's cigarettes and bring them to school, and we'd smoke them at playtime in the shelter under the woodwork classroom. We called it Smokers' Corner.

It was daft really. I didn't even like smoking, it gives me headaches. But I joined in cos all the others did. Well, I didn't want Arthur Boocock picking on me.

We took it in turns to stand guard. I liked it when it was my turn, it meant I didn't have to join in the smoking.

Smokers' Corner was at the top end of the play-ground, opposite the girls' school. That's how I first saw Janis. It was one playtime. I was on guard, when I saw these three girls staring at me from an upstairs window. They kept laughing and giggling. I didn't take much notice, which was a good job cos I saw Melrose coming across the playground with Mr Rush-ton, the deputy head. I ran into the shelter and warned the lads.

'Arthur, Tony – Melrose and Rushton are coming!'

There was no way we could've been caught. We knew we could get everything away before Melrose or Rushton or anybody could reach us, even if they ran across the playground as fast as they could. We had a plan you see.

First, everybody put their cigarettes out – not on the ground – with their fingers. It didn't half hurt if you didn't wet them enough. Then Arthur would open a little iron door that was in the wall next to the boiler house. Norbert had found it ages ago. It must've been there for years. Tony reckoned it was some sort of oven. Anyway, we'd empty our pockets and put all the cigarettes inside. All the time we'd be waving our hands about to get rid of the smoke, and Arthur would squirt the fresh-air spray he'd nicked from home. Then we'd shut the iron door and start playing football or tig.

Melrose never let on why he used to come storming across the playground. He never said anything, but we knew he was trying to catch the Smokers – and he knew we knew. All he'd do was give us all a look in turn, and march off. But on that day, the day those girls had been staring and giggling at me, he did say something.

'Watch it! All of you. I know what you're up to. Just watch it. 'Specially you, Boocock.'

We knew why Melrose picked on Arthur Boocock.

'You're running for the school on Saturday, Boocock. You'd better win or I'll want to know the reason why.'

Mr Melrose is in charge of athletics, and Arthur holds the school record for the mile. Melrose reckons he could run for Yorkshire one day, if he trains hard enough.

I didn't like this smoking lark, it made me cough, gave me a headache, and I was sure we'd get caught one day.

'Hey, Arthur, we'd better pack it in. Melrose is going to catch us one of these days.'

Arthur wasn't bothered.

'Ah you! You're just scared, you're yeller!'

Yeah, I was blooming scared.

'I'm not. I just think he's going to catch us.'

Then Arthur did something that really shook me. He took his right hand out of his blazer pocket – for a minute I thought he was going to hit me, but he didn't. He put it to his mouth instead, and blew out some smoke. He's mad. He'd kept his cigarette in his hand – in his pocket – all the time. He's mad. I didn't say anything though. I was scared he'd thump me.

On my way home after school that day, I saw those girls. They were standing outside Wilkinson's sweetshop, and when they saw me they started giggling again. They're daft, girls. They're always giggling. One of them, the tallest, was ever so pretty though. The other two were all right, but not as pretty as the tall girl. It was the other two that were doing most of the giggling.

'Go on, Glenda, ask him.'

'No, you ask him.'

'No, you're the one who wants to know. You ask him.'

'Shurrup!'

The tall one looked as embarrassed as I felt. I could see her name written on her school-bag – Janis Webster.

The other two were still laughing, and telling each other to ask me something. I could feel myself going red. I didn't like being stared at.

'Do you two want a photograph or summat?'

They giggled even more.

'No, thank you, we don't collect photos of monkeys, do we, Glenda?'

The one called Glenda stopped laughing and gave the other one a real dirty look.

'Don't be so rude, Christine.'

Then, this Christine started teasing her friend Glenda.

'Ooh, just cos you like him, Glenda Bradshaw, just cos you fancy him.'

I started walking away. Blimey! If any of the lads came by and heard this going on, I'd never hear the end of it. The one called Christine started shouting after me.

'Hey, my friend Glenda thinks you're ever so nice. She wants to know if you want to go out with her.'

Blimey! Why did she have to shout so the whole street could hear? I looked round to make sure nobody like Arthur Boocock, or Norbert or Tony was about. I didn't want them to hear these stupid lasses saying things like that. I mean, we didn't go out with girls, because . . . well . . . we just didn't.

I saw the pretty one, Janis, pulling Christine's arm. She was telling her to stop embarrassing me. She was nice, that Janis, much nicer than the other two. I mean, if I was forced to go out with a girl, you know if somebody said, 'You will die tomorrow if you don't go out with a girl,' then I wouldn't have minded going out with Janis Webster. She was really nice.

I often looked out for her after that, but when I saw her, she was always with the other two. The one time I did see her on her own, I was walking home with Tony and Norbert and I'd pretended I didn't know her – even though she'd smiled and said hello. 'Course, I sometimes used to see her at playtime, when it was my turn to stand guard at Smokers' Corner. I liked being on guard twice as much now. As well as not having to smoke, it gave me a chance to see Janis. She was smashing. I couldn't get her out of my mind. I was always thinking about her, you know, having day-dreams. I was forever 'rescuing' her.

One of my favourite rescues was where she was

being bullied by about half a dozen lads, not hitting her or anything, just mucking about. And one of them was always Arthur Boocock. And I'd go up very quietly and say, 'Are these lads bothering you?' And before she had time to answer, a fight would start, and I'd take them all on. All six at once, and it would end up with them pleading for mercy. And then Janis would put her hand on my arm and ask me to let them off . . . and I would – that was my favourite rescue.

That's how the trouble with Arthur Boocock started.

I'd been on guard one playtime, and had gone into one of my 'rescues'. It was the swimming-bath rescue. Janis would be swimming in the deep end, and she'd get into trouble, and I'd dive in and rescue her. I'd bring her to the side, put a towel round her, and then walk off without saying a word. Bit daft really, because I can't swim. Not a stroke. Mind you, I don't suppose I could beat up six lads on my own either, 'specially if one of them was Arthur Boocock. Anyway, I was just pulling Janis out of the deep end when I heard Melrose shouting his head off.

'Straight to the Headmaster's study – go on, all three of you!'

I looked round, and I couldn't believe it. Melrose was inside Smokers' Corner. He'd caught Arthur, Tony and Norbert. He was giving Arthur a right crack over the head. How had he caught them? I'd been there all the time . . . standing guard . . . thinking about Janis . . . I just hadn't seen him coming . . . oh heck . . .

'I warned you, Boocock – all of you. Go and report to the Headmaster!'

As he was going past me, Arthur showed me his fist. I knew what that meant.

They all got the cane for smoking, and Melrose really had it in for Arthur even though he was still doing well at his running. The more Melrose picked on Arthur, the worse it was for me, cos Arthur kept beating me up.

That was the first thing he'd done after he'd got the cane – beat me up. He reckoned I'd not warned them about Melrose on purpose.

'How come you didn't see him? He's blooming big enough.'

'I just didn't.'

I couldn't tell him that I'd been day-dreaming about Janis Webster.

'He must've crept up behind me.'

Arthur hit me, right on my ear.

'How could he go behind you? You had your back to the wall. You did it on purpose, you yeller-belly!'

And he hit me again, on the same ear.

After that, Arthur hit me every time he saw me. Sometimes, he'd hit me in the stomach, sometimes on the back of my neck. Sometimes, he'd raise his fist and I'd think he was going to hit me, and he'd just walk away, laughing. Then he started taking my spending money. He'd say, 'Oh, you don't want that, do you?' and I'd say, 'No, you have it, Arthur.'

I was really scared of him. He made my life a misery. I dreaded going to school, and when I could, I'd stay at home by pretending to be poorly. I used to stick my fingers down my throat and make myself sick.

I suppose that's when I started to get behind with my school-work, but anything was better than being bullied by that rotten Arthur Boocock. And when I did go to school, I'd try to stay in the classroom at playtime, or I'd make sure I was near the teacher who was on playground duty. 'Course, Arthur thought it was all very funny, and he'd see if he could hit me without the teacher seeing – and he could.

Dinner-time was the worst because we had an hour free before the bell went for school dinners, and no one was allowed to stay inside. It was a school rule. That was an hour for Arthur to bully me. I used to try and hide but he'd always find me.

By now it didn't seem to have anything to do with him being caught smoking and getting the cane. He just seemed to enjoy hitting me and tormenting me. So I stopped going to school dinners. I used to get some chips, or a Cornish pasty, and wander around.

Sometimes, I'd go into town and look at the shops, or else I'd go in the park and muck about. Anything to get away from school and Arthur Boocock.

That's how I met Archie.

There's a running-track in the park, a proper one with white lines and everything, and one day I spent all dinner-time watching this old bloke running round. That was Archie. I went back the next day and he was there again, running round and round, and I got talking to him.

'Hey, mister, how fast can you run a mile?'

I was holding a bag of crisps, and he came over and took one. He grinned at me.

'How fast can *you* run a mile?'

I'd never tried running a mile.

'I don't know, I've never tried.'

He grinned again.

'Well, now's your chance. Come on, get your jacket off.'

He was ever so fast and I found it hard to keep up with him, but he told me I'd done well. I used to run with Archie every day after that. He gave me an old track-suit top, and I'd change into my shorts and pumps, and chase round the track after him. Archie said I was getting better and better.

'You'll be running for Yorkshire one of these days.'

I laughed and told him to stop teasing me. He gave me half an orange. He always did after running.

'Listen, lad, I'm serious. It's all a matter of training. Anybody can be good if they train hard enough. See you tomorrow.'

That's when I got the idea.

I decided to go in for the mile in the school sports at the end of term. You had to be picked for everything else, but anybody could enter the mile.

There were three weeks to the end of term, and in that three weeks I ran everywhere. I ran to school. I ran with Archie every dinner-time. I went back and ran on the track after school. Then I'd run home. If my mum wanted anything from the shops, I'd run there. I'd get up really early in the mornings and run before breakfast. I was always running. I got into tons of trouble at school for not doing my homework properly, but I didn't care. All I thought about was the mile.

I had day-dreams about it. Always me and Arthur, neck and neck, and Janis would be cheering me on. Then I dropped Janis from my day-dreams. She wasn't important any more. It was just me and Arthur against each other. I was sick of him and his bullying.

Arthur did well at sports day. He won the high-jump and the long-jump. He was picked for the half-mile and the four-forty, and won them both. Then, there was the announcement for the mile.

'Will all those competitors who wish to enter the open mile, please report to Mr Melrose at the start.'

I hadn't let on to anybody that I was going to enter, so everybody was very surprised to see me when I went over in my shorts and pumps – especially Melrose. Arthur thought it was hilarious.

'Well, look who it is. Do you want me to give you half a mile start?'

I ignored him, and waited for Melrose to start the race. I surprised a lot of people that day, but nobody more than Arthur. I stuck to him like a shadow. When he went forward, I went forward. If he dropped back, I dropped back. This went on for about half the race. He kept giving me funny looks. He couldn't understand what was happening.

'You won't keep this up. Just watch.'

And he suddenly spurted forward. I followed him, and when he looked round to see how far ahead he was, he got a shock when he saw he wasn't.

It was just like my day-dreams. Arthur and me neck and neck, the whole school cheering us on, both of us heading for the last bend. I looked at Arthur and saw the tears rolling down his cheeks. He was crying his eyes out. I knew at that moment I'd beaten him. I don't mean I knew I'd won the race. I wasn't bothered about that. I knew I'd beaten *him* – *Arthur*. I knew he'd never hit me again.

That's when I walked off the track. I didn't see any point in running the last two hundred yards. I suppose that's because I'm not a natural athlete.

Daddy-Long-Legs

JEAN WEBSTER

As Noel Streatfeild's girls in *Ballet Shoes* are taken up and cared for by generosity of the absent Great-Uncle Ma y, so the American orphan Jerusha Abbe from the John Grier Home is sent to col thanks to a benefactor who wishes to remain anonymous. All that Jerusha knows of him is a glimpse she had of his shadow as he left the orphanage, thrown up by his car's headlights as he waved to it, looking 'for all the world, like a huge, wavering daddy-long-legs'.

Jerusha is coming up to sixteen and, at first, when writing the regular letters which her benefactor has demanded she send him, she tells this mysterious man:

*

I have been thinking about you a great deal this summer; having somebody take an interest in me after all these years makes me feel as though I have found a sort of family. It seems as though I belong to somebody now, and it's a very comfortable sensation. I must say, however, that when I think about you, my imagination has very little to work upon. There are just three things that I know:

I. You are tall.

II. You are rich.

III. You hate girls.

I suppose I might call you Dear Mr Girl-Hater. Only that's sort of insulting to me. Or Dear Mr Rich-Man, but that's insulting to you, as though money were the only important thing about you . . . So I've decided to call you Dear Daddy-Long-Legs. I hope you won't mind. It's just a private pet name – we won't tell Mrs Lippett.

Through Jerusha's letters to Daddy-Long-Legs we learn about her life as she goes through college and as she grows and eventually falls in love. It's a funny, moving book – first published in 1912.

October 10th

Dear Daddy-Long-Legs,

Did you ever hear of Michael Angelo?

He was a famous artist who lived in Italy in the Middle Ages. Everybody in English Literature seemed to know about him, and the whole class laughed because I thought he was an archangel. He sounds like an archangel, doesn't he? The trouble with college is that you are expected to know such a lot of things you've never learned. It's very embarrassing at times. But now, when the girls talk about things that I never heard of, I just keep still and look them up in the encyclopedia.

I made an awful mistake the first day. Somebody mentioned Maurice Maeterlinck, and I asked if she was a freshman. That joke has gone all over college. But anyway, I'm just as bright in class as any of the others – and brighter than some of them!

Do you care to know how I've furnished my room? It's a symphony in brown and yellow. The wall was tinted buff, and I've bought yellow denim curtains and cushions and a mahogany desk (second-hand for three dollars) and a rattan chair and a brown rug with an ink spot in the middle. I stand the chair over the spot.

The windows are up high; you can't look out from an ordinary seat. But I unscrewed the looking-glass from the back of the bureau, upholstered the top and moved it up against the window. It's just the right height for a window-seat. You pull out the drawers like steps and walk up. Very comfortable!

Sallie McBride helped me choose the things at the senior auction. She has lived in a house all her life and knows about furnishing. You can't imagine what fun it is to shop and pay with a real five-dollar bill and get some change – when you've never had more than a few cents in your life. I assure you, Daddy dear, I do appreciate that allowance.

Sallie is the most entertaining person in the world – and Julia Rutledge Pendleton the least so. It's queer what a mixture the registrar can make in the matter of room-mates. Sallie thinks everything is funny – even flunking – and Julia is bored at everything. She never makes the slightest effort to be amiable. She believes that if you are a Pendleton, that fact alone admits you to heaven without any further examination. Julia and I were born to be enemies.

And now I suppose you've been waiting very impatiently to hear what I am learning?

I. *Latin*: Second Punic war. Hannibal and his forces pitched camp at Lake Trasimenus last night. They prepared an ambuscade for the Romans, and a battle took place at the fourth watch this morning. Romans in retreat.

II. *French*: 24 pages of *The Three Musketeers* and third conjugation, irregular verbs.

III. *Geometry*: Finished cylinders; now doing cones.

IV. *English*: Studying exposition. My style improves daily in clearness and brevity.

V. *Physiology*: Reached the digestive system. Bile and the pancreas next time. Yours, on the way to being educated,

Jerusha Abbott

PS I hope you never touch alcohol, Daddy? It does dreadful things to your liver.

October 25th

Dear Daddy-Long-Legs,

I've made the basketball team and you ought to see the bruise on my left shoulder. It's blue and mahogany with little streaks of orange. Julia Pendleton tried for the team, but she didn't get in. Hooray!

You see what a mean disposition I have.

College gets nicer and nicer. I like the girls and the teachers and the classes and the campus and the things to eat. We have ice-cream twice a week and we never have cornmeal mush.

You only wanted to hear from me once a month, didn't you? And I've been peppering you with letters every few days! But I've been so excited about all these new adventures that I *must* talk to somebody; and you're the only one I know. Please excuse my exuberance; I'll settle pretty soon. If my letters bore you, you can always toss them into the waste-basket.

I promise not to write another till the middle of November.

Yours most loquaciously,

Judy Abbott

December 19th

Dear Daddy-Long-Legs,

You never answered my question and it was very important.

ARE YOU BALD?

I have it planned exactly what you look like – very satisfactorily – until I reach the top of your head, and then I *am* stuck. I can't decide whether you have white hair or black hair or sort of sprinkly grey hair or maybe none at all.

I've drawn your portrait, but the problem is, shall I add some hair?

Would you like to know what colour your eyes are? They're grey, and your eyebrows stick out like a porch roof (beetling, they're called in novels), and your mouth is a straight line with a tendency to turn down at the corners. Oh, you see, I know! You're a snappy old thing with a temper.

(Chapel bell.)

9.45 p.m.

I have a new unbreakable rule: never, never to study at night no matter how many written reviews are coming in the morning. Instead, I read just plain books – I have to, you know, because there are eighteen blank years behind me. You wouldn't believe, Daddy, what an abyss of ignorance my mind is; I am just realizing the depths myself. The things that most girls with a properly assorted family and a home and friends and a library know by absorption, I have never heard of. For example:

I never read *Mother Goose* or *David Copperfield* or *Ivanhoe* or *Cinderella* or *Bluebeard* or *Robinson Crusoe* or *Jane Eyre* or *Alice in Wonderland* or a word of Rudyard Kipling. I didn't know that Henry the Eighth was married more than once or that Shelley was a poet. I didn't know that people used to be monkeys and that the Garden of Eden was a beautiful myth. I didn't know that R.L.S. stood for Robert Louis Stevenson or that George Eliot was a lady. I had never seen a picture of the Mona Lisa and (it's true but you won't believe it) I had never heard of Sherlock Holmes.

Now, I know all of these things and a lot of others besides, but you can see how much I need to catch up. And oh, but it's fun! I look forward all day to evening, and then I put an 'engaged' on the door and get into my nice red bathrobe and furry slippers and

91

pile all the cushions behind me on the couch, and light the brass student lamp at my elbow, and read and read and read. One book isn't enough. I have four going at once. Just now, they're Tennyson's poems and *Vanity Fair* and Kipling's *Plain Tales* and – don't laugh – *Little Women*. I find that I am the only girl in college who wasn't brought up on *Little Women*. I haven't told anybody though (that *would* stamp me as queer). I just quietly went and bought it with $1.12 of my last month's allowance; and the next time somebody mentions pickled limes, I'll know what she is talking about!

(Ten o'clock bell. This is a very interrupted letter.)

March 26th

Mr D. L. L. Smith,

Sir: You never answer any questions; you never show the slightest interest in anything I do. You are probably the horridest one of all those horrid trustees, and the reason you are educating me is not because you care a bit about me, but from a sense of duty.

I don't know a single thing about you. I don't even know your name. It is very uninspiring writing to a thing. I haven't a doubt but that you throw my letters into the waste-basket without reading them. Hereafter I shall write only about work.

My re-examinations in Latin and geometry came last week. I passed them both and am now free from conditions.

Yours truly,

Jerusha Abbott

April 2nd

Dear Daddy-Long-Legs,

I am a BEAST.

Please forget about that dreadful letter I sent you last week – I was feeling terribly lonely and miserable and sore-throaty the night I wrote. I didn't know it, but I was just sickening for tonsillitis and grippe and lots of things mixed. I'm in the infirmary now, and have been here for six days; this is the first time they would let me sit up and have a pen and paper. The head nurse is *very bossy*. But I've been thinking about it all the time and I shan't get well until you forgive me.

I've drawn a picture of the way I look, with a bandage tied around my head in rabbit's ears.

Doesn't that arouse your sympathy? I am having sublingual gland swelling. And I've been studying physiology all the year without ever hearing of sublingual glands. How futile a thing is education!

I can't write any more; I get rather shaky when I sit

up too long. Please forgive me for being impertinent and ungrateful. I was badly brought up.

Yours with love,

Judy Abbott

May 30th

Dear Daddy-Long-Legs,

I have been walking and talking and having tea with a man. And with a very superior man – with Mr Jervis Pendleton of the House of Julia; her uncle, in short (in long, perhaps I ought to say; he's as tall as you). Being in town on business, he decided to run out to the college and call on his niece. He's her father's youngest brother, but she doesn't know him very intimately. It seems he glanced at her when she was a baby, decided he didn't like her, and has never noticed her since.

Anyway, there he was, sitting in the reception room very proper with his hat and stick and gloves beside him; and Julia and Sallie with seventh-hour recitations that they couldn't cut. So Julia dashed into my room and begged me to walk him about the campus and then deliver him to her when the seventh hour was over. I said I would, obligingly but unenthusiastically, because I don't care much for Pendletons.

But he turned out to be a sweet lamb. He's a real

human being – not a Pendleton at all. We had a beautiful time; I've longed for an uncle ever since. Do you mind pretending you're my uncle? I believe they're superior to grandmothers.

Mr Pendleton reminded me a little of you, Daddy, as you were twenty years ago. You see, I know you intimately, even if we haven't ever met!

He's tall and thinnish with a dark face all over lines, and the funniest underneath smile that never quite comes through but just wrinkles up the corners of his mouth. And he has a way of making you feel right off as though you'd known him a long time. He's very companionable.

We walked all over the campus from the quadrangle to the athletic grounds; then he said he felt weak and must have some tea. He proposed that we go to College Inn – it's just off the campus by the pine walk. I said we ought to go back for Julia and Sallie, but he said he didn't like to have his nieces drink too much tea; it made them nervous. So we just ran away and had tea and muffins and marmalade and ice-cream and cake at a nice little table out on the balcony. The inn was quite conveniently empty, this being the end of the month and allowances low.

We had the jolliest time! But he had to run for his train the minute he got back and he barely saw Julia at all. She was furious with me for taking him off; it seems he's an unusually rich and desirable uncle. It relieved my mind to find he was rich, for the tea and things cost sixty cents apiece.

This morning (it's Monday now) three boxes of chocolates came by express for Julia and Sallie and me. What do you think of that? To be getting candy from a man!

I begin to feel like a girl instead of a foundling.

I wish you'd come and have tea some day and let me see if I like you. But wouldn't it be dreadful if I didn't? However, I know I should.

Bien! I make you my compliments.

'*Jamais je ne t'oublierai.*'

Judy

PS I looked in the glass this morning and found a perfectly new dimple that I'd never seen before. It's very curious. Where do you suppose it came from?

March 5th

Dear Daddy-Long-Legs,

There is a March wind blowing, and the sky is filled with heavy, black moving clouds. The crows in the pine trees are making such a clamour! It's an intoxicating, exhilarating, *calling* noise. You want to close your books and be off over the hills to race with the wind.

We had a paper chase last Saturday over five miles of squashy cross-country. The fox (composed of three girls and a bushel or so of confetti) started half an hour before the twenty-seven hunters. I was one of the twenty-seven; eight dropped by the wayside; we ended nineteen. The trail led over a hill, through a cornfield, and into a swamp where we had to leap lightly from hummock to hummock. Of course half of us went in ankle deep. We kept losing the trail, and we wasted twenty-five minutes over that swamp. Then up a hill through some woods and in at a barn window! The barn doors were all locked and the window was up high and pretty small. I don't call that fair, do you?

But we didn't go through; we circumnavigated the barn and picked up the trail where it issued by way of a low shed roof on to the top of a fence. The fox thought he had us there, but we fooled him. Then straight away over two miles of rolling meadow, and awfully hard to follow, for the confetti was getting sparse. The rule is that it must be at the most six feet apart, but they were the longest six feet I ever saw. Finally, after two hours of steady trotting, we tracked Monsieur Fox into the kitchen of Crystal Spring (that's a farm where the girls go in bob-sleighs and hay-wagons for chicken and waffle suppers) and we found the three foxes placidly eating milk and honey and biscuits. They hadn't thought we would get that far; they were expecting us to stick in the barn window.

Both sides insist that they won. I think we did, don't you? Because we caught them before they got back to the campus. Anyway, all nineteen of us settled like locusts over the furniture and clamoured for honey. There wasn't enough to go round, but Mrs Crystal Spring (that's our pet name for her; she's by rights a Johnson) brought up a jar of strawberry jam and a can of maple syrup – just made last week – and three loaves of brown bread.

We didn't get back to college till half-past six – half an hour late for dinner – and we went straight in without dressing, and with perfectly unimpaired appetites! Then we all cut evening chapel, the state of our boots being enough of an excuse.

I never told you about examinations. I passed everything with the utmost ease – I know the secret now, and am never going to fail again. I shan't be able to graduate with honours though, because of that beastly Latin prose and geometry freshman year. But I don't care. Wot's the hodds so long as you're 'appy? (That's a quotation. I've been reading the English classics.)

Speaking of classics, have you ever read *Hamlet*? If you haven't, do it right off. It's *perfectly corking*. I've been hearing about Shakespeare all my life, but I had no idea he really wrote so well; I always suspected him of going largely on his reputation.

I have a beautiful play that I invented a long time ago when I first learned to read. I put myself to sleep every night by pretending I'm the person (the most important person) in the book I'm reading at the moment.

At present I'm Ophelia – and such a sensible Ophelia! I keep Hamlet amused all the time, and pet him and scold him and make him wrap up his throat when he has a cold. I've entirely cured him of being melancholy. The King and Queen are both dead – an accident at sea; no funeral necessary – so Hamlet and I are ruling in Denmark without any bother. We have the kingdom working beautifully. He takes care of the governing, and I look after the charities. I have just founded some first-class orphan asylums. If you or any of the other trustees would like to visit them, I shall be pleased to show you through. I think you might find a great many helpful suggestions.

I remain, sir, yours most graciously,

Ophelia,
Queen of Denmark

Lock Willow,
June 19th

Dear Daddy-Long-Legs,

I'm educated! My diploma is in the bottom bureau drawer with my two best dresses. Commencement was as usual, with a few showers at vital moments. Thank you for your rose-buds. They were lovely. Master Jervie and Master Jimmie both gave me roses, too, but I left theirs in the bath-tub and carried yours in the class procession.

Here I am at Lock Willow for the summer — for ever maybe. The board is cheap; the surroundings quiet and conducive to a literary life. What more does a struggling author wish? I am mad about my book. I think of it every waking moment, and dream of it at night. All I want is peace and quiet and lots of time to work (interspersed with nourishing meals).

Master Jervie is coming up for a week or so in August, and Jimmie McBride is going to drop in sometime through the summer. He's connected with a bond house now, and goes about the country selling bonds to banks. He's going to combine the Farmers' National at the Corners and me on the same trip.

You see that Lock Willow isn't entirely lacking in society. I'd be expecting to have you come motoring through — only I know now that that is hopeless.

When you wouldn't come to my commencement, I tore you from my heart and buried you for ever.

Judy Abbott, AB

August 27th

Dear Daddy-Long-Legs,

Where are you, I wonder?

I never know what part of the world you are in, but I hope you're not in New York during this awful weather. I hope you're on a mountain peak (but not in Switzerland; somewhere nearer) looking at the snow and thinking about me. Please be thinking about me. I'm quite lonely and I want to be thought about. Oh, Daddy, I wish I knew you! Then when we were unhappy we could cheer each other up.

I don't think I can stand much more of Lock Willow. I'm thinking of moving. Sallie is going to do settlement work in Boston next winter. Don't you think it would be nice for me to go with her, then we could have a studio together? I could write while she *settled* and we could be together in the evenings. Evenings are very long when there's no one but the Semples and Carrie and Amasai to talk to. I know in advance that you won't like my studio idea. I can read your secretary's letter now:

Miss Jerusha Abbott.

Dear Madam,

Mr Smith prefers that you remain at Lock Willow.

Yours truly,

   Elmer H. Griggs

I hate your secretary. I am certain that a man named Elmer H. Griggs must be horrid. But truly, Daddy, I think I shall have to go to Boston. I can't stay here. If something doesn't happen soon, I shall throw myself into the silo pit out of sheer desperation.

Mercy! but it's hot. All the grass is burnt up and the brooks are dry and the roads are dusty. It hasn't rained for weeks and weeks.

This letter sounds as though I had hydrophobia, but I haven't. I just want some family.

Goodbye, my dearest Daddy.

I wish I knew you.

   Judy

The Boy from New York City

MARCEL FEIGEL

Up to date again, but still about an American.

As well as including published favourites in a collection, it's good to have something brand-new to show. I am proud that Marcel Feigel's story should be having its first publication in this book. Its realism and humour show that the business of someone new coming to the school can be a time of trial for everyone, for the newcomer and for the rest.

A New Kid in School

I'll never forget the first time I saw him.

He suddenly appeared in class one day, wearing jeans, a black jumper and sun-glasses. He walked in as if he had just bought the school. And the word quickly got around that he was the boy from New York City.

For some reason he sat next to me. I felt honoured because there were more than a few empty seats in the room so he had quite a choice. But I quickly realized that it wasn't me, it was probably the fact that I sat at the back, in the last row.

But if he thought he could escape attention by sitting at the back, he was wrong. It might have made it a little harder for everybody because it meant they had to turn around, but that didn't stop the kids in my class. And of course whenever they turned to look at him, they had to look at me. Which made me feel a bit like a star, even though I knew it wasn't really me they were interested in.

Our teacher, Mr Martin, was also curious. But he showed it in a different way.

'Do you need those glasses for medical reasons?' he asked.

The new boy shook his head.

'Then I'd appreciate it if you didn't wear them in class.'

'Why's that, teach?' the boy from New York City asked.

'My name is not "teach", it's Mr Martin. Is that clear?'

'Sure thing, teach, I mean . . . Mr Martin.'

'And the reason I'd like you to take them off is that I like to look at your eyes when I'm speaking to you.'

The new boy looked at him for a few seconds and we all wondered what he was going to do. Then he took them off, gave a big smile and said, 'That's cool.'

Sal

His name was Sal. Sal Rivera. And it didn't take long for Sal and I to become friends.

Sal lived in Manhattan. On West 96th Street, on the 28th floor. That seemed incredibly high to me but he said it was nothing special. 'You go in some buildings,' he said, 'like the Pan Am or the Empire State, and the elevator [lift] goes straight up to the 50th floor without stopping. And that's just as a way of saying hello. Then you press the floor you want, like 84 or 96.'

It seemed to me as if everything in New York was in numbers. Even the schools were numbered. Sal went to PS 98, which stood for Public School 98. Over there all the public schools are state schools. When I told him that public schools here were posh schools where you had to pay quite a lot of money in school fees, he just shook his head. 'You people are really weird,' he said. 'What's the point of calling it a public school if it's really private.'

He said in his school you heard almost as much Spanish as you did English.

'That sounds like fun,' I said

'Well, it is in a way,' Sal answered. 'But it can also get pretty rough. Because you get a lot of kids from different backgrounds and sometimes they have trouble getting along.'

I wasn't quite sure what he meant.

'Well . . . put it like this,' he said. 'There are some pretty heavy dudes, out there. And some of them can get into some *serious* trouble,' and he really emphasized the word 'serious'. As he talked his own face turned serious as if he was remembering some of the things he had seen.

'Are you a heavy dude?' I asked jokingly.

He gave me a strange look that seemed to come from far away. Then he said, 'Sometimes.'

An American Comes to Tea

A few weeks after Sal arrived I asked him if he'd like to come for tea after school. 'Sure thing,' he said.

Sal was very polite when he came over. He took his 'shades' off before entering the house and quietly sat down at the table. Though he seemed surprised when Mum came in with the teapot. He looked like he'd never seen one before.

'Don't you drink tea in New York?' I asked.

'Only when I'm sick,' he said.

'Well, never mind,' my mum said. 'You're in England now, where people drink tea when they're healthy.'

'What would you normally have after school?' I asked.

'A big slice of pepperoni pizza and a root beer,' he said, and you could see that just thinking about it made his mouth water.

'Well, it's obvious that you've never had a cup of proper tea,' Mum said, pouring him out a cup. 'There,' she said, 'how does that taste?'

Sal took a sip and said, 'Real cool.'

Mum suddenly looked worried. 'Oh, isn't it hot enough? I'm sure I boiled the water.'

'No problem,' Sal said. 'It's fine.'

'"Cool" is just an expression, Mum,' I said. 'Like "great" or "fab" or, as Uncle Don says, "groovy".'

'Oh, *that* man,' Mum said, making an exasperated face. 'He's still living in the sixties.'

'My dad was around in the sixties,' Sal said. 'He was in San Francisco, where he says it was really *happening*.'

'Really,' Mum said. 'And where is it happening now?'

Sal looked serious for a minute. 'I don't know. But I just hope it happens somewhere when I get older. So I can tell my kids about it.'

'Well, you can tell them about the time you were in England,' Mum said.

'And drank tea,' I added.

Sal smiled. 'That's right, this is happening, isn't it?'

'Sometimes,' Mum said, 'you only realize something was happening long after it happened.' And then she poured us another cup of tea.

Mr Martin Assigns a Report

About two weeks after Sal arrived Mr Martin said we had to do a project on New York. I don't know whether Sal's arrival had anything to do with his choice – it may be that he was going to assign it anyway – but I've a funny feeling that it just might have.

'Now you don't have to do it on New York City,' he said. 'If you prefer, you can do it on New York State.'

'What's the difference?' Adrian asked.

'I know they both have the same name,' Mr Martin said, 'which can make it a little confusing . . .'

'You can say that again, teach . . . I mean, Mr Martin,' Sal chimed in. 'There's a lot of confused people out there.'

'But what you've got to remember,' Mr Martin continued, 'is that New York City is part of New York State.'

'Which is the capital?' Digby asked.

'Neither,' Mr Martin said.

'That's no help,' Adrian said, covering his face with his hand, which is what he always did when he didn't know what was going on.

'Nor to me,' George added.

Now it was Carol's turn. 'You mean,' she said, 'if I was sending a letter to Sal over there, I would have to send it to New York, New York?'

'Correct,' Mr Martin said. 'It's just like the song says: "New York, New York, so good they named it twice." Now I want all of you to go and do some research and find out as much as you can about your subject. And if you have any questions, just ask Sal, he'll help you out.'

Sal seemed really taken aback by what Mr Martin said. 'Hey, hold on a minute,' he said. 'I may live there, but when it comes to knowing about the place . . . I mean history and stuff, that's not really my . . .'

'Don't be so modest, Sal,' Mr Martin said with a

very cheeky smile. And I think he quite enjoyed putting Sal on the spot.

The Baddest of the Bad

One day Sal was showing us pictures of some of his buddies from New York. They all seemed to look like Sal. They dressed the same way and they all seemed to have the same kind of look.

'That's Vito,' he said, 'he and I play basketball together, and this is Julio, my neighbour, and that's Lou, he's a real clown, and this here is Ira, he's real smart.' And he went along like that until he got to one picture when he suddenly stopped and stared at it for a minute.

'Who's that?' George asked.

'That's my friend De Witt, and I tell you, he's baaaad,' Sal said, shaking his head.

'You mean, he's naughty,' Adrian said.

'No, you got it wrong. You see where I come from bad is good. Because to be bad means that you're really cool. So if everybody goes around saying, "Woh, that dude is bad," then he's really somebody.'

Sal looked around and saw we were all looking puzzled but at the same time we were trying hard to keep up with him. I wondered if it was like that with teachers when they're trying to explain a point and the class isn't really with them.

'Let me get this right,' Digby said, scratching his head. 'Bad is good. Is that right?'

'You got it,' Sal said. 'But there's bad and there's bad. Now you can get some dude and he's bad and that's pretty good, but if he's *really* bad then you've got to stretch it out a bit like, "Woh, that boy is baaaaaad." You got that?'

I think we were finally beginning to understand. Even Digby was blinking a little less than he was a minute ago.

Now it was Freddie's turn. 'Then the best is really the worst,' he said.

'Sorry, Freddie, I don't get you,' Sal said.

'I mean,' Freddie said, 'if you say that someone is the worrrst,' and he tried giving the word the kind of emphasis that Sal would, 'then he must really be the best.'

'No, no,' Sal said. 'There is no worst. You mean the baddest.'

Now we were all puzzled again. 'The "baddest", what's that?' Digby asked.

'That sounds like it's incorrect,' Adrian added.

'The baddest,' Sal said patiently, 'is the best. It's the ultimate. The king. It is being supercool. Now you guys got that?' He looked at us to make sure we understood.

We all nodded.

Adrian couldn't hold in his excitement any more. He threw up his arms and shouted, 'I WANT TO BE BAD.'

'How bad?' Sal asked.

'THE BADDEST!' we all answered together.

Sal smiled. 'Well, all I can say is you guys got a long way to go. But you keep trying,' he said encouragingly, 'and one day you will be.'

Sal Stops a Thief

We were just coming back into the classroom after playtime when I notice that there was someone in the classroom already. It could have been just another student but there was something slightly suspicious about this boy. He seemed too big to be in that room.

Sal noticed it too. 'Who's that?' he asked. 'I don't think I've seen him before. Hey,' he shouted. 'What class are you in?'

The boy was taken by surprise. He looked at us but didn't answer. Perhaps he was trying to figure out what to say.

At the same time Mr Penrose, the headmaster, was passing by. He looked into the room, saw the boy, and said, 'Are you sure you're in the right room?'

Now the boy was really startled. He knew he had to say something. 'Er ... I ... I ... must have ... gone into ...'

I could see that Mr Penrose was becoming suspicious. 'Excuse me, I'm not sure I know you,' he said in his most headmasterly manner. 'What's your name?'

The boy was now cornered. He quickly looked around him but there was no one to help. 'Smith,' he said, 'Dickie Smith.'

'I don't think we have a Dickie Smith here,' Mr Penrose said.

By now quite a few of the students had come in from the playground and were gathered outside the classroom, curious to see what was going on. 'I know I don't have the memory I used to possess,' Mr Penrose went on, 'but I do believe I know most of the students in my school and I don't have any recollection ...'

While Mr Penrose was talking, Dickie Smith was looking down at the floor as if he was inspecting his trainers.

'... of having seen you here before,' Mr Penrose continued. 'Do you know my name?' he asked.

Dickie Smith had stopped inspecting his trainers, and was now shuffling from one foot to the other. Then he did a strange thing. He took a step forward. Then another. Then, before any of us knew what happened, he was out the door, into the hallway, only a few feet from where Mr Penrose stood.

And then he suddenly made a run for it.

It all happened so quickly that we were completely taken by surprise. And before anyone had a chance to react, he rocketed down the hall and had such a head start that no one had a chance of possibly catching him. Or so we thought.

But what we hadn't counted on was Sal.

He suddenly took off in hot pursuit. And if Dickie Smith had been like a rocket, then Sal was like a bullet.

Although the older boy had the height and longer legs, as well as the advantage of surprise, we soon saw that Sal had the speed. And the determination.

Meanwhile Mr Penrose was yelling, 'Stop that boy, don't let that boy leave the school.' But nobody was paying much attention. By now the whole school seemed to have heard there was something going on and they were all standing in the hallway watching what seemed to us like the race of the century.

Sal had started off a long way behind and had an awful lot of ground to make up, but he was catching up very quickly. It probably helped that everybody was cheering him on. 'C'mon, Sal,' they were yelling, and, 'Go get him,' as if it was Sports Day. Even the teachers were shouting.

He had managed to cut down a very long lead and

he was now crouched right behind the taller boy, breathing down his neck, ready to overtake him.

The older boy knew what was happening but there wasn't much he could do. He tried desperately to lunge forward but by now Sal was right beside him.

Suddenly he threw himself against the older boy and, using all his weight as well as his momentum, flung him against the wall. At the same time he yelled in a voice that surprised us all because it didn't sound like him, 'Up against the wall, Jack. And no funny stuff.'

That was it. Dickie Smith knew he was beaten. He suddenly went limp, as if all the fight had gone out of his body. And he very obediently spread both his arms against the wall over his head just like Sal motioned him to. And when Sal yelled, 'Higher,' he did just as he was told.

After Sal got him in the position that he wanted, he said, 'That's it, now hold it right there.' Then he emptied Dickie's pockets and, sure enough, six pens fell out, along with a watch and two rings. Then, for the first time, Sal looked behind him and saw Mr Penrose followed by two teachers lumbering along.

None of us had ever seen anything like it before. Except perhaps on the telly. And I don't think any of us got over what we saw. But I think what amazed us more than anything else was the change that had come over Sal. Because this was definitely not the Sal we knew.

'Mr Penrose,' he said very coolly, when the head-master finally arrived on the scene, 'he's all yours. I don't think he'll give you any trouble.'

Even Mr Penrose was respectful. 'Thanks, Sal,' he said. 'I think we can take over now. Well done.'

Then Sal turned around and walked back towards his classmates. But now he was walking very slowly, as if it had only just dawned on him what he'd been through. By the time he rejoined us he was the same old Sal again.

Adrian was the first to speak. 'That was pretty awesome, Sal.'

Digby was even more enthusiastic. 'Sal, that was absolutely magnificent,' he said.

'Hey, that's nothin',' Sal answered. 'You guys ought to see the scrapes we get into back home.'

'Where did you learn all that?' Bette asked, looking all dewy-eyed.

Now Sal was smiling. He was enjoying his moment of glory. 'Hey, don't you guys go to the movies?' he said.

'Yeah, sure,' we all agreed and laughed. But I knew that you don't learn that kind of stuff from watching movies. And I think everybody else knew the same thing as well. But we didn't say anything. Because there was nothing else to say really.

By this time Mr Penrose had returned and was saying, 'Everybody back in the classroom.' And we all wandered back in, as if it was just another day.

A Singing Lesson

One day we were talking in the playground when Digby asked, 'What kind of music do people like in New York?'

'We like all kinds,' Sal answered, 'but me and my buddies, we like to sing Doo-Wop.'

'"Dwop", I never heard of that,' George said, looking puzzled. 'What is "dwop" music?'

'Doo-Wop,' Sal corrected him. 'It's street-corner singing. I learned it from my Uncle Diego. He used to sing on 7th Street and Avenue B with a bunch of guys. He sang bass. He told me that when he was a kid every street corner had its own singing group. And that wasn't just New York. You found them in Baltimore, Chicago, Detroit – all the big cities. Some of the groups even became famous, like the Moon-glows.'

'Is it difficult?' Adrian asked.

'Nah, it's easy,' Sal said. 'All you do is get a bunch of guys and you all stand around like this:'

He made us all stand in a semicircle and he stood in the middle. And we all started singing:

> *Din Din Di Din Din*
> *Din Din Di Din Din*
> *Din Din Din Din Da*

Then we all brought our voices up, one octave at a time:

> *da*
> *Da*
> *DA*

Then Sal came in with:

> *Love you like I do*

And we all went:

> *WOP*

But the *WOP* had to be just right. We had to come in at the exact second. Then we had to cut it off – just like that, it had to be really sharp.

'It's all in the timing,' Sal said. And he was right. But we soon got the hang of it. And it wasn't long before we were Doo-Wopping, and Shawadda-ing and Bop-Sha-Bopping and Ring-A-Ding-Donging as if we had been doing it for years. Sal was getting excited and saying, 'Hey, you guys are doing real good, keep it up,' when suddenly Mr Penrose came by. We were so wrapped up in our singing that we didn't even notice him.

He paused for a minute to listen, then looked at us and said, 'I wish you would put in as much effort practising for the Christmas concert.'

The Reports

Finally the day came for the reports.

'All right,' Mr Martin said, 'let's see how much you have all learned about New York. Who did it used to belong to?'

'The English,' Adrian said.

'And before that?'

'The Dutch,' Carol answered.

'And before that?'

'The Spanish,' Freddie said.

'No, it belonged to the only true native Americans. Now who would that be?'

'The Indians,' Digby volunteered.

'Correct,' Mr Martin said. 'And the Dutch bought Manhattan from them. Anybody know for how much?'

'A million dollars?' Carol said.

'Oh, a lot less than that,' Mr Martin said. A few others guessed but we were all way off the mark. 'I think I'd better tell you,' he said finally. 'For all of Manhattan Island the Dutch paid the princely sum of . . . twenty-four dollars. And do you know how much it's worth now?'

'Five dollars,' Sal said, and everybody laughed.

'I think it's a bit more than that,' Mr Martin said. 'Why, just one square, like Rockefeller Plaza, can be worth over a billion dollars.'

'That's a lot of zeros,' Sal said.

'You can say that again,' Mr Martin said, 'although here we call them "noughts". Does anyone know just how many there are in a billion?' And he walked over to the blackboard and wrote $1,000,000,000. 'That's a thousand million, which I think you'll all agree is considerably more than twenty-four dollars. But don't forget that twenty-four dollars was worth an awful lot more then than it is now, and that if you had invested that small sum a few centuries ago, you'd have quite a nice little nest-egg of several million now. But to go back to the Dutch, after they bought Manhattan, what did they call it – anyone know?'

Claire raised her hand. 'New Amsterdam,' she said.

'Correct,' Mr Martin said. 'And it was run by a Dutchman called Peter Stuyvesant, who, if anyone is interested, only had one leg. He became the mayor. And so it remained until the British snatched it away from him and renamed it New York. Now, let's hear a few reports.'

So then we all got up in turn and gave our reports. And after each one Mr Martin would look over to the back of the room and say, 'Did you know that, Sal?'

And Sal would say, 'Unh unh, that's news to me, teach . . . I mean, Mr Martin.'

After all the reports were delivered, including mine on Monticello, which was the home of Thomas Jefferson, third president of the United States, Mr Martin said, 'Well done, everybody, you've all done a splendid job. I've learned a few things and I dare say so has our esteemed visitor, to whom I will leave the last word. Is there anything you'd like to say, Sal?'

'I think you've all done a real good job,' Sal said. 'And when I go back, which is pretty soon, I'm gonna know more about the place than anybody else, including the mayor.'

An Apple for a Special Student

We were all taken by surprise by Sal's announcement, mostly because we hadn't heard him say anything about leaving before. But then we all knew it had to happen sometime. Afterwards Sal told me that he didn't really want to go, not just yet. But his father had come on business for a few months, and now his business was finished, and it was time to go home.

Once we knew he was going, everyone in the class agreed that we had to throw a leaving party. But we wanted to make it a surprise.

Mr Martin knew about it of course. And he was just as keen on the idea as the rest of us.

But it wasn't that easy keeping it a secret from Sal. Because the only way we could plan the party was in school. And Sal was always there. In fact, the few times we did manage to huddle together and do a little planning, Sal would always come over, because he didn't like being left out of anything. 'Hey, what's going on?' he'd say. And we'd have to change the conversation and quickly talk about something else.

It got so bad that in the end we had to organize it from my home. Adrian and I were in charge. Then we got Digby in because he didn't like being left out. Then Freddie started feeling hurt. And since we didn't want to limit it to just boys, Bette and Carol joined us. And before we knew it the whole class was involved.

We decided to have it on Sal's final day because we wanted to give him a last day that he wouldn't forget.

The first thing we did was to turn the whole classroom into New York. We had a replica of the Empire State Building on one side of the room. And behind it we managed to fill in the rest of the New York skyline. Then on the other side of the room we had the Statue of Liberty, as well as loads of posters. And everyone in the class wore an 'I LOVE NY' T-shirt.

We all managed to get into the classroom early so that when Sal arrived, he found us already sitting in our seats.

He came in, took one look, did a double take because he didn't believe what he was seeing, looked again, then smiled and shook his head very slowly. 'You guys are something else,' he said. And we knew we'd made it because that's the highest compliment Sal gives out.

Then Mr Martin stepped in. 'Sal, as you know, usually it's the students who are supposed to give the teacher an apple. But in this case the process has been reversed. All your class-mates have banded together to give you the largest apple they could find – the Big Apple.'

The rest of the morning we spent discussing New York or the Big Apple as New Yorkers call it. It wasn't like giving our reports. We expressed our own feelings. Mr Martin asked us if we wanted to go there and why. 'And please don't say it's because you want to visit Sal.'

It turned out that everyone wanted to go there. Because we had all seen it so often in movies and on the telly. And we felt as if we knew the place already.

'You can all come over and stay at my place,' Sal said.

'I'm not so sure your parents would appreciate that,' Mr Martin said.

In the afternoon we had a party. We had popcorn and root beer because that was Sal's favourite soft drink. And my mum baked a cherry-pie because she knew that Sal liked that as well. And Carol went to a special

American shop where she bought pretzels and special cream-filled biscuits called Oreos and corn chips. And everybody else brought in the usual stuff you get at parties. And we all had a real feast.

Then, about an hour before it was time to go, George brought in a cassette player and put on an old song he'd found called 'The Boy from New York City'.

At the same time everybody got up and we all formed a circle around Sal and we began singing to the music.

The boys started it off:

Badoom Doom Doom Doom Doom Doom Doom
Oooah Oooah Oooah Kitty
Tell us about the boy from New York City

Then the girls came in:

He's kind of tall
He's really fine
Someday I hope to make him
Mine all mine

Sal loved it. He was smiling from ear to ear, swaying to the music and clapping his hands. 'Hey, I'm not going to forget this,' he said. 'You guys have laid on a party and a half.

'And I'll tell you something else,' he said. 'I'm gonna miss you.'

And we miss him too. Because the boy from New York City wasn't just cool and he wasn't just bad. He was extra cool. And most definitely the baaadest.

The Choice is Yours

JAN MARK

Jan Mark used to teach in a school just a playing-field away from where I worked. We never met in those youthful days, but every word Jan has ever written about life in school shouts her real experience across at me.

Here she presents the classic choice: the should-I-do-this or should-I-do-that, to please this or that teacher, neither of whom can see any point of view but their own? It's from her 1980 volume of short stories *Nothing to be Afraid Of*, which was highly commended for the Carnegie Medal.

The music-room was on one side of the quadrangle and the changing-room faced it on the other. They were linked by a corridor that made up the

third side, and the fourth was the view across the playing-fields. In the music-room Miss Helen Francis sat at the piano, head bent over the keyboard as her fingers tittuped from note to note, and swaying back and forth like a snake charming itself. At the top of the changing-room steps Miss Marion Taylor stood, sportively poised with one hand on the doorknob and a whistle dangling on a string from the other; quivering with eagerness to be out on the field and inhaling fresh air. They could see each other. Brenda, standing in the doorway of the music-room, could see them both.

'Well, come in, child,' said Miss Francis. 'Don't *haver*. If you must haver, don't do it in the doorway. Other people are trying to come in.'

Brenda moved to one side to make way for the other people, members of the choir who would normally have shoved her out of the way and pushed past. Here they shed their school manners in the corridor and queued in attitudes of excruciated patience. Miss Helen Francis favoured the noiseless approach. Across the quadrangle the under-thirteen hockey eleven roistered, and Miss Marion Taylor failed to intervene. Miss Francis observed all this with misty disapproval and looked away again.

'Brenda dear, are you coming in, or going out, or putting down roots?'

The rest of the choir was by now seated: first

sopranos on the right, second sopranos on the left, thirds across one end and Miss Humphry, who was billed as an alto but sang tenor, at the other. They all sat up straight, as trained by Miss Francis, and looked curiously at Brenda, who should have been seated too, among the first sopranos. Her empty chair was in the front row, with the music stacked on it, all ready. Miss Francis cocked her head to one side like a budgerigar that sees a millet spray in the offing.

'Have you a message for us, dear? From above?' She meant the headmistress, but by her tone it could have been God and his angels.

'No, Miss Francis.'

'From *beyond*?'

'Miss Francis, can I ask – ?'

'You *may* ask, Brenda. Whether or not you *can* is beyond my powers of divination.'

Brenda saw that the time for havering was at an end.

'Please, Miss Francis, may I be excused from choir?'

The budgie instantly turned into a marabou stork.

'Excused, Brenda? Do you have a pain?'

'There's a hockey practice, Miss Francis.'

'I am aware of that.' Miss Francis cast a look, over her shoulder and across the quadrangle, that should have turned Miss Taylor to stone, and the under-thirteen eleven with her. 'How does it concern you, Brenda? How does it concern me?'

'I'm in the team, Miss Francis, and there's a match on Saturday,' said Brenda.

'But, my dear —' Miss Francis smiled at her with surpassing sweetness. 'I think my mind must be going.' She lifted limp fingers from the keyboard and touched them to her forehead, as if to arrest the absconding mind. 'Hockey practices are on Tuesdays and Fridays. Choir practices are on Mondays and Thursdays. It was ever thus. Today is Thursday. Everyone else thinks it's Thursday, otherwise they wouldn't be here.' She swept out a spare arm that encompassed the waiting choir, and asked helplessly, 'It *is* Thursday, isn't it? You all think it's Thursday? It's not just me having a little brainstorm?'

The choir tittered, *sotto voce*, to assure Miss Francis that it was indeed Thursday, and to express its mass contempt for anyone who was fool enough to get caught in the cross-fire between Miss Francis and Miss Taylor.

'It's a match against the High School, Miss Francis. Miss Taylor called a special practice,' said Brenda, hoping that her mention of the High School might save her, for if Miss Francis loathed anyone more than she loathed Miss Taylor, it was the music mistress at the High School. If the match had been against the High School choir, it might have been a different matter, and Miss Francis might have been out on the sidelines chanting with the rest of them: 'Two — four — six — eight, who — do — we — hate?'

Miss Francis, however, was not to be deflected. 'You know that I do not allow any absence from choir without a very good reason. Now, will you sit down, please?' She turned gaily to face the room. 'I think we'll begin with the Schubert.'

'Please. May I go and tell Miss Taylor that I can't come?'

Miss Francis sighed a sigh that turned a page on the music-stand.

'Two minutes, Brenda. We'll wait,' she said venomously, and set the metronome ticking on the piano so that they might all count the two minutes, second by second.

Miss Taylor still stood upon the steps of the changing-room. While they were all counting, they could turn round and watch Brenda tell Miss Taylor that she was not allowed to attend hockey practice.

Tock.

Tock.

Tock.

Brenda closed the door on the ticking and began to run. She would have to run to be there and back in two minutes, and running in the corridors was forbidden.

Miss Taylor had legs like bath loofahs stuffed into long, hairy grey socks, that were held up by tourniquets of narrow elastic. When she put on her stockings after school and mounted her bicycle to pedal strenuously home up East Hill, you could still see the twin red marks, like the rubber seals on Kilner jars. The loofahs were the first things that Brenda saw as she mounted the steps, and the grey socks bristled with impatience.

'Practice begins at twelve fifty,' said Miss Taylor. 'I suppose you were thinking of joining us?'

Brenda began to cringe all over again.

'Please, Miss Taylor, Miss Francis says I can't come.'

'Does she? And what's it got to do with Miss Francis? Are you in detention?'

'No, Miss Taylor. I'm in choir.'

'You may only be the goalkeeper, Brenda, but we still expect you to turn out for practices. You'll have to explain to Miss Francis that she must manage without you for once. I don't imagine that the choir will collapse if you're missing.'

'No, Miss Taylor.'

'Go on, then. At the double. We'll wait.'

Brenda ran down the steps, aware of the music-room windows but not looking at them, and back into the corridor. Half-way along it she was halted by a shout from behind.

'*What* do you think you're doing?'

Brenda turned and saw the Head Girl, Gill Rogers, who was also the school hockey captain and had the sense not to try and sing as well.

'Running, Gill. Sorry, Gill.'

'Running's forbidden. You know that. Go back and walk.'

'Miss Taylor told me to run.'

'It's no good trying to blame Miss Taylor; I'm sure she didn't tell you to run.'

'She said "at the double",' said Brenda.

'That's not the same thing at all. Go back and *walk*.'

Brenda went back and walked.

'Two minutes and fifteen seconds,' said Miss Francis, reaching for the metronome, when Brenda finally got back to the music-room. 'Sit down quickly, Brenda. Now then – I said sit down, Brenda.'

'Please, Miss Francis –'

A look of dire agony appeared on Miss Francis's face – it could have been wind so soon after lunch – and she held the metronome in a strangler's grip.

'I think you've delayed us long enough, Brenda.'

'Miss Taylor said couldn't you please excuse me from choir just this once as it's such an important match,' said Brenda, improvising rapidly, since Miss Taylor had said nothing of the sort. Miss Francis raised a claw.

'I believe I made myself perfectly clear the first time. Now, sit down, please.'

'But they're all waiting for me.'

'So are we, Brenda. I must remind you that it is not

common practice in this school to postpone activities for the sake of Second-year girls. What position do you occupy in the team? First bat?' Miss Francis knew quite well that there are no bats required in a hockey game, but her ignorance suggested that she was above such things.

'Goalkeeper, Miss Francis.'

'Goalkeeper? From the fuss certain persons are making, I imagined that you must be at least a fast bowler. Is there no one else in the lower school to rival your undoubted excellence at keeping goal?'

'I *did* get chosen for the team, Miss Francis.'

'Clearly you have no equal, Brenda. That being the case, you hardly need to practise, do you?'

'Miss Taylor thinks I do,' said Brenda.

'Well, I'm afraid I don't. I would never, for one moment, keep you from a match, my dear, but a practice on a *Thursday* is an entirely different matter. Sit down.'

Brenda, panicking, pointed to the window. 'But she won't start without me.'

'Neither will I. You may return very quickly and tell Miss Taylor so. At once.'

Brenda set off along the corridor, expecting to hear the first notes of 'An die Musik' break out behind her. There was only silence. They were still waiting.

'Now run and get changed,' said Miss Taylor, swinging her whistle, as Brenda came up the steps again. 'We've waited long enough for you, my girl.'

'Miss Francis says I can't come,' Brenda said, baldly.

'Does she, now?'

'I've got to go back.' A scarcely suppressed jeer rose from the rest of the team, assembled in the changing-room.

'Brenda, this is the under-thirteen eleven, not the under-thirteen ten. There must be at least sixty of you in that choir. Are you really telling me that your absence will be noticed?'

'Miss Francis'll notice it,' said Brenda.

'Then she'll just have to notice it,' said Miss Taylor under her breath, but loudly enough for Brenda to hear and appreciate. 'Go and tell Miss Francis that I insist you attend this practice.'

'Couldn't you give me a note, please?' said Brenda. Miss Taylor must know that any message sent via Brenda would be heavily edited before it reached its destination. She could be as insulting as she pleased in a note.

'A note?' Brenda might have suggested a dozen red roses thrown in with it. 'I don't see any reason to send a note. Simply tell Miss Francis that on this occasion she must let you go.'

Brenda knew that it was impossible to tell Miss Francis that she must do anything, and Miss Taylor knew it too. Brenda put in a final plea for mercy.

'Couldn't *you* tell her?'

'We've already wasted ten minutes, Brenda, while you make up your mind.'

'You needn't wait –'

'When I field a team, I field a team; not ten-elevenths of a team.' She turned and addressed the said team. 'It seems we'll have to stay here a little longer,' her eyes strayed to the music-room windows, 'while Brenda arrives at her momentous decision.'

Brenda turned and went down the steps again.

'Hurry *up*, girl.'

Miss Taylor's huge voice echoed dreadfully round the confining walls. She should have been in the choir herself, singing bass to Miss Humphry's tenor. Brenda began to run, and like a cuckoo from a clock, Gill Rogers sprang out of the cloakroom as she cantered past.

'Is that you again?'

Brenda side-stepped briskly and fled towards the music-room, where she was met by the same ominous silence that had seen her off. The choir, cowed and bowed, crouched over the open music sheets and before them, wearing for some reason her *indomitable* expression, sat Miss Francis, tense as an overwound clockwork mouse and ready for action.

'At last. Really, Brenda, the suspense may prove too much for me. I thought you were never coming back.' She lifted her hands and brought them down sharply on the keys. The choir jerked to attention. An over-eager soprano chimed in and then subsided as Miss Francis raised her hands again and looked round. Brenda was still standing in the doorway.

'Please sit down, Brenda.'

Brenda clung to the doorpost and looked hopelessly at Miss Francis. She would have gone down on her knees if there had been the slightest chance that Miss Francis would be moved.

'Well?'

'Please, Miss Francis, Miss Taylor says I *must* go to the practice.' She wished devoutly that she were at home where, should rage break out on this scale, someone would have thrown something. If only Miss Francis would throw something; the metronome, perhaps, through the window.

Tock . . . tock . . . tock . . . *CRASH*! Tinkle tinkle.

But Miss Francis was a lady. With tight restraint she closed the lid of the piano.

'It seems,' she said, in a bitter little voice, 'that we are to have no music today. A hockey game is to take precedence over a choir practice.'

'It's *not* a game,' said Brenda. 'It's a practice, for a match. Just this once . . . ?' she said, and was disgusted to find a tear boiling up under her eyelid. 'Please, Miss Francis.'

'No, Brenda. I do not know why we are enduring this ridiculous debate [Neither do I, Miss Francis], but

I thought I had made myself quite clear the first time you asked. You will not miss a scheduled choir practice for an unscheduled hockey practice. Did you not explain to Miss Taylor?'

'Yes I did!' Brenda cried. 'And she said you wouldn't miss me.'

Miss Francis turned all reasonable. 'Miss you? But my dear child, of course we wouldn't miss you. No one would miss you. You are not altogether indispensable, are you?'

'No, Miss Francis.'

'It's a matter of principle. I would not dream of abstracting a girl from a hockey team, or a netball team, or even, heaven preserve us, from a shove-ha'penny team, and by the same token I will not allow other members of staff to disrupt my choir practices. Is that clear?'

'Yes, Miss Francis.'

'Go and tell Miss Taylor. I'm sure she'll see my point.'

'Yes, Miss Francis.' Brenda turned to leave, praying that the practice would at last begin without her, but the lid of the piano remained shut.

This time the Head Girl was waiting for her and had her head round the cloakroom door before Brenda was fairly on her way down the corridor.

'Why didn't you come back when I called you, just now?'

Brenda leaned against the wall and let the tear escape, followed by two or three others.

'Are you crying because you've broken rules,' Gill demanded, 'or because you got caught? I'll see you outside the Sixth-form Room at four o'clock.'

'It's not my fault.'

'Of course it's your fault. No one forced you to run.'

'They're making me,' said Brenda, pointing two-handed in either direction, towards the music-room and the changing-room.

'I dare say you asked for it,' said Gill. 'Four o'clock, please,' and she went back into the senior cloakroom in the hope of catching some malefactor fiddling with the locks on the lavatory doors.

This last injustice gave Brenda a jolt that she might otherwise have missed, and the tears of self-pity turned hot with anger. She trudged along to the changing-room.

'You don't exactly hurry yourself, do you?' said Miss Taylor. 'Well?'

'Miss Francis says I can't come to hockey, Miss Taylor.'

Miss Taylor looked round at the restive members of the under-thirteen eleven and knew that for the good of the game it was time to make a stand.

'Very well, Brenda, I must leave it to you to make up your mind. Either you turn out now for the

practice or you forfeit your place in the team. Which
is it to be?'

Brenda looked at Miss Taylor, at the music-room
windows, and back to Miss Taylor.

'If I leave now, can I join again later?'

'Good Lord. Is there no end to this girl's cheek?
Certainly not. This is your last chance, Brenda.'

It would have to be the choir. She could not bear
to hear the singing and never again be part of it,
Thursday after Monday, term after term. If you missed
a choir practice without permission, you were ejected
from the choir. There was no appeal. There would be
no permission.

'I'll leave the team, Miss Taylor.'

She saw at once that Miss Taylor had not been
expecting this. Her healthy face turned an alarming
colour, like Lifebuoy kitchen soap.

'Then there's nothing more to say, is there? This
will go on your report, you understand. I cannot be
bothered with people who don't take things seriously.'

She turned her back on Brenda and blew the whistle
at last, releasing the pent-up team from the changing-
room. They were followed, Brenda noticed, by Pat
Stevens, the reserve, who had prudently put on the
shin-pads in advance.

Brenda returned to the music-room. The lid of
the piano was still down and Miss Francis's brittle
elbow pinned it.

'The prodigal returns,' she announced to the choir as Brenda entered, having seen her approach down the corridor. 'It is now one fifteen. May we begin, dear?'

'Yes, Miss Francis.'

'You finally persuaded Miss Taylor to see reason?'

'I told her what you said.'

'And?'

'She said I could choose between missing the choir practice and leaving the team.'

Miss Francis was transformed into an angular little effigy of triumph.

'I see you chose wisely, Brenda.'

'Miss Francis?'

'By coming back to the choir.'

'No, Miss Francis . . .' Brenda began to move towards the door, not trusting herself to come any closer to the piano. 'I'm going to miss choir practice. I came back to tell you.'

'Then you will leave the choir, Brenda. I hope you understand that.'

'Yes, Miss Francis.'

She stepped out of the room for the last time and closed the door. After a long while she heard the first notes of the piano, and the choir finally began to sing. Above the muted voices a whistle shrilled, out on the playing-field. Brenda went and sat in the junior cloakroom, which was forbidden in lunch-hour, and cried. There was no rule against that.

The Mouth-organ Boys

James Berry

Whether in a northern city in Britain or a country village in Jamaica, most children in school are driven by the same need to belong.

This story – from the Smarties Prize-winning collection *A Thief in the Village* – has that poetic grip of truth that says, *I know about this*, that hallmark of the sensitive writer who recognizes that children all over the world are experts about their own lives and friendships, at home and at school, and who will know how he felt because he – and they – are not the only ones . . .

I wanted a mouth–organ, I wanted it more than anything else in the whole world. I told my mother. She kept ignoring me, but I still wanted a mouth-organ badly.

THE
MOUTH
ORGAN
BOYS

I was only a boy. I didn't have a proper job. Going to school was like a job, but nobody paid me to go to school. Again I had to say to my mother, 'Mam, will you please buy a mouth-organ for me?'

It was the first time, now, that my mother stood and answered me properly. Yet listen to what my mother said. 'What d'you want a mouth-organ for?'

'All the other boys have a mouth-organ, Mam,' I told her.

'Why is that so important? You don't have to have something just because others have it.'

'They won't have me with them without a mouth-organ, Mam,' I said.

'They'll soon change their minds, Delroy.'

'They won't, Mam. They really won't. You don't know Wildo Harris. He never changes his mind. And he never lets any other boy change his mind either.'

'Delroy, I haven't got the time to argue with you. There's no money to buy a mouth-organ. I bought your new shoes and clothes for Independence celebrations. Remember?'

'Yes, Mam.'

'Well, money doesn't come on trees.'

'No, Mam.' I had to agree.

'It's school-day. The sun won't stand still for you. Go and feed the fowls. Afterwards milk the goat. Then get yourself ready for school.'

She sent me off. I had to go and do my morning jobs.

Oh, my mother never listened! She never understood anything. She always had reasons why she
couldn't buy me something and it was no good
wanting to talk to my dad. He always cleared off to
work early.

All my friends had a mouth-organ, Wildo, Jim,
Desmond, Len – everybody had one, except me. I
couldn't go round with them now. They wouldn't let
anybody go round with them without a mouth-organ.
They were now 'The Mouth-organ Boys'. And we
used to be all friends. I used to be their friend. We all
used to play games together, and have fun together.
Now they pushed me away.

'Delroy! Delroy!' my mother called.

I answered loudly. 'Yes, Mam!'

'Why are you taking so long feeding the fowls?'

'Coming, Mam.'

'Hurry up, Delroy.'

Delroy. Delroy. Always calling Delroy!

I milked the goat. I had breakfast. I quickly brushed
my teeth. I washed my face and hands and legs. No
time left and my mother said nothing about getting
my mouth-organ. But my mother had time to grab
my head and comb and brush my hair. She had time
to wipe away toothpaste from my lip with her hand. I
had to pull myself away and say, 'Good day, Mam.'

'Have a good day, Delroy,' she said, staring at me.

I ran all the way to school. I ran wondering if the

Mouth-organ Boys would let me sit with them today. Yesterday they didn't sit next to me in class.

I was glad the boys came back. We all sat together as usual. But they teased me about not having a mouth-organ.

Our teacher, Mr Goodall, started writing on the blackboard. Everybody was whispering. And it got to everybody talking quite loudly. Mr Goodall could be really cross. Mr Goodall had big muscles. He had a moustache too. I would like to be like Mr Goodall when I grow up. But he could be really cross. Suddenly Mr Goodall turned round and all the talking stopped, except for the voice of Wildo Harris. Mr Goodall held the chalk in his hand and stared at Wildo Harris. He looked at Teacher and dried up. The whole class giggled.

Mr Goodall picked out Wildo Harris for a question. He stayed sitting and answered.

'Will you please stand up when you answer a question?' Mr Goodall said.

Wildo stood up and answered again. Mr Goodall ignored him and asked another question. Nobody answered. Mr Goodall pointed at me and called my name. I didn't know why he picked on me. I didn't know I knew the answer. I wanted to stand up slowly, to kill time. But I was there, standing. I gave an answer.

'That is correct,' Mr Goodall said.

147

I sat down. My forehead felt hot and sweaty, but I felt good. Then in the school yard at recess time, Wildo joked about it. Listen to what he had to say: 'Delroy Brown isn't only a big head. Delroy Brown can answer questions with a big mouth.'

'Yeah!' the gang roared, to tease me.

Then Wildo had to say, 'If only he could get a *mouth*-organ.' All the boys laughed and walked away.

I went home to lunch and as usual I came back quickly. Wildo and Jim and Desmond and Len were together, at the bench, under the palm tree. I went up to them. They were swapping mouth-organs, trying out each one. Everybody made sounds on each mouth-organ, and said something. I begged Len, I begged Desmond, I begged Jim, to let me try out their mouth-organs. I only wanted a blow. They just carried on making silly sounds on each other's mouth-organs. I begged Wildo to lend me his. He didn't even look at me.

I faced Wildo. I said, 'Look. I can do something different as a Mouth-organ Boy. Will you let me do something different?'

Boy, everybody was interested. Everybody looked at me.

'What different?' Wildo asked.

'I can play the comb,' I said.

'Oh, yeah,' Wildo said slowly.

'Want to hear it?' I asked. 'My dad taught me how to play it.'

'Yeah,' Wildo said. 'Let's hear it.' And not one boy smiled or anything. They just waited.

I took out my comb. I put my piece of tissue-paper over it. I began to blow a tune on my comb and had to stop. The boys were laughing too much. They laughed so much they staggered about. Other children came up and laughed too. It was all silly, laughing at me.

I became angry. Anybody would get mad. I told them they could keep their silly Mouth-organ Boys business. I told them it only happened because Desmond's granny gave him a mouth-organ for his birthday. And it only caught on because Wildo went and got a mouth-organ too. I didn't sit with the boys in class that afternoon. I didn't care what the boys did.

I went home. I looked after my goats. Then I ate. I told my mum I was going for a walk. I went into the centre of town where I had a great surprise.

The boys were playing mouth-organs and dancing. They played and danced in the town square. Lots of kids followed the boys and danced around them.

It was great. All four boys had the name 'The Mouth-organ Boys' across their chests. It seemed they did the name themselves. They cut out big coloured letters for the words from newspapers and magazines. They gummed the letters down on a strip of brown paper, then they made a hole at each end of the paper. Next a string was pushed through the holes, so they could tie the names round them. The boys looked great. What a super name: 'The Mouth-organ Boys'! How could they do it without me!

'Hey, boys!' I shouted, and waved. 'Hey, boys!' They saw me. They jumped up more with a bigger act, but ignored me. I couldn't believe Wildo, Jim, Desmond and Len enjoyed themselves so much and didn't care about me.

I was sad, but I didn't follow them. I hung about the garden railings, watching. Suddenly I didn't want to watch any more. I went home slowly. It made me sick how I didn't have a mouth-organ. I didn't want to eat. I didn't want the lemonade and bun my mum gave me. I went to bed.

Mum thought I wasn't well. She came to see me. I didn't want any fussing about. I shut my eyes quickly. She didn't want to disturb me. She left me alone. I opened my eyes again.

If I could drive a truck I could buy loads of mouth-organs. If I was a fisherman I could buy a hundred mouth-organs. If I was an aeroplane pilot I could buy truck-loads of mouth-organs. I was thinking all those things and didn't know when I fell asleep.

Next day at school the Mouth-organ Boys sat with me. I didn't know why but we just sat together and joked a little bit. I felt good running home to lunch in the usual bright sunlight.

I ran back to school. The Mouth-organ Boys were

under the palm tree, on the bench. I was really happy. They were really unhappy and cross and this was very strange.

Wildo grabbed me and held me tight. 'You thief!' he said.

The other boys came around me. 'Let's search him,' they said.

'No, no!' I said. 'No.'

'I've lost my mouth-organ and you have stolen it,' Wildo said.

'No,' I said. 'No.'

'What's bulging in your pocket, then?'

'It's mine,' I told them. 'It's mine.'

The boys held me. They took the mouth-organ from my pocket.

'It's mine,' I said. But I saw myself up to Headmaster. I saw myself getting caned. I saw myself disgraced.

Wildo held up the mouth-organ. 'Isn't this red mouth-organ mine?'

'Of course it is,' the boys said.

'It's mine,' I said. 'I got it at lunch-time.'

'Just at the right time, eh?' Desmond said.

'Say you borrowed it,' Jim said.

'Say you were going to give it back,' Len said.

Oh, I had to get a mouth-organ just when Wildo lost his! 'My mother gave it to me at lunch-time,' I said.

'Well, come and tell Teacher,' Wildo said.

The bell rang. We hurried to our class. My head was aching. My hands were sweating. My mother would have to come to school, and I hated that.

Wildo told our teacher I stole his mouth-organ. It was no good telling Teacher it was mine, but I did. Wildo said his mouth-organ was exactly like that. And I didn't have a mouth-organ.

Mr Goodall went to his desk. And Mr Goodall brought back Wildo's grubby red mouth-organ. He said it was found on the floor.

How could Wildo compare his dirty red mouth-organ with my new, my beautiful, my shining-clean mouth-organ? Mr Goodall made Wildo Harris say he was sorry.

Oh it was good. It was good to become one of 'The Mouth-organ Boys'.

First Communion

GER DUFFY

Church schools are a bit different, and Catholic schools more different than most in their links with formal Instruction into the Faith.

Ger Duffy writes tellingly about a crucial time in Ann Doyle's life when she stands up for herself against school and against home. The story comes from a 1990 feminist collection, *School Daze*.

They were late. The tiled corridors were empty. As they crept up the stairs, the chanting of multiplication tables and singing followed them. Tricia disappeared through her classroom door. Ann walked more slowly.

'. . . three four five six, I slept late, seven eight nine, the car wouldn't start.'

Her excuses seemed feeble. The smells of wax polish and chalk filled her nose as she entered the classroom. Sister Ignatius looked up from calling the register and frowned.

Since the Christmas holidays Sr. Ignatius had been drilling the class in the catechism they, as first communicants, were expected to know. She walked back and forth across the front of the room, her stick, placed at an upward angle, pointed at the class. At first the questions were easy. Who made the world? Who is God? What are the Ten Commandments? Recite the creed. Ann still hadn't been asked. Six girls were already standing in the corner, for every answer missed they would receive two slaps on each hand. Ann tried to remember the creed.

'I believe in God the Father Almighty Maker of Heaven and Earth, Maker of all things something and something.'

Claire Hensey recited it perfectly. When Ann's turn arrived, the finger jumped over her.

'I'm not going to bother with girls who come in late.'

That evening, Ann went to Mrs Digan's to get fitted for her communion dress. While she waited in the hall, she could hear people talking behind the partition. Mam sat down as they waited, occasionally she pulled at the collar of her dress. Tricia delved through a mound of scrap material in a heap at the corner; although she had made her first communion the year before, she too was getting a new dress for the occasion. At last, the Larkins appeared from behind the partition and left. The partition was made out of chipboard; at one end stood a huge, old mirror, framed in dark wood. On ledges along the wall were packets of pins, measuring tape, rolls of velcro, ribbons and linings. In the mirror, everyone looked broader and squarer than they really were. Mrs Digan hurried back, rushing through the curtained entrance so that it billowed after her. In the hall people coughed and shuffled their feet. The material had been cut and tacked together hurriedly and looked the size and shape of brown-paper grocery bags. Trisha's was pink and Ann's was blue, turquoise blue, a name she'd never heard before, and Trisha's was cerise pink, Mrs Digan told them, pins clamped between her lips.

Since last month when the *Parish Bulletin* had stated that girls would not be restricted to wearing white for the first communion ceremony, Mam had pored over the heavy dressmaking books in Mrs Digan's back room and examined all the shades and textures of the material in Melville's drapery shop. Eventually she decided on a heavy crimplene material with white daisy trimming. Ann looked in the mirror. One sleeve was sewn on, the dress was held together with tacking and pins. She looked odd in it, half dressed. Ann didn't believe for one moment that this was going to be her first communion dress, and even if Mam was serious, there was Tricia's white dress from last year, though Tricia was smaller and fatter than her and Mam had said that Ann looked spindly in it.

At night, in the red-spotted darkness behind her lids, she saw herself in Tricia's dress, gliding slowly to the altar. She felt the weight and awe of the veil on her head and the crown of plastic flowers intertwined. Somewhere Sr. Ignatius was looking on approvingly saying, 'What a pious little girl Ann Doyle is, how strange I never noticed it before!'

In the run-up to the big day, Sr. Ignatius grew more and more excited. Hardly a day passed without everyone in the class receiving a slap. Ordinary subjects were forgotten. Catechism took from nine until two. The girls sat upright in the two-by-two desks. Gradually the pressure increased. Those who hesitated were removed from the line. Carmel Kilklein licked both hands furtively before being slapped, then ran back to her seat grinning, although her hands were tucked under her armpits. The class grew hot and sweaty, waiting to be asked. The Bracken twins created a diversion by fainting simultaneously and, when they recovered, vomiting all over their jumpers. Sr. Ignatius scattered sawdust at their feet. Although it was cold, they had to stand in their blouses, in front of the class, dishonoured. Just then a precise knock was heard. Sr. Ignatius warned the class.

'*Cuineas anios.*' [Quiet now.]

The door was almost closed, the sharp tones of the Monsignor contrasted with the lighter tones of the nun. Anyone who failed the oral examination would have to stay back a year and couldn't make their first communion until then. The Monsignor entered, followed by Sr. Ignatius. She clapped her hands.

'What do you say, girls?'

'Good morning, Monsignor,' they chorused.

'Good morning, girls,' he snapped. 'A little bird told me you are all very hard-working girls, is that true?'

Mary Sherlock nodded and said, 'Yes, Monsignor.'

'Hmn, we'll see. I'm sure you all know your catechism very well indeed by now.' He stopped and looked at the twins.

'Dear oh dear, what have we here at all?'

'They were ill just as you arrived, Monsignor,' Sr. Ignatius stated, her hands clasped.

'Would you like to go home, girls?' he barked. They shook their heads shyly.

'They are from the country, Monsignor, they will get the school bus home. Sit down, girls.' They walked stiffly from the spot and sat in their desks.

'I hope you're not frightened of me,' he said with a laugh that stopped short.

'Of course not,' Sr. Ignatius laughed in return.

'Well. Does anyone know the Lord's prayer?'

Every hand shot up, some even waved. Annette Daly stood up and said it, her hands devoutly pressed together.

'Well, Sister, I think because they've all been so good, we can let them have the rest of the day off.'

A confused buzz ran through the class. The questions they'd learnt every night and recited every morning hung on their tongues. Ann ran home by herself for the first time ever.

Mam stood in the kitchen ironing.

'Why are you home so early?'

'We had the catechism exam, I ran all the way home, what's for dinner?'

Ann rummaged in her bag for the school note from Sr. Ignatius, asking parents to ensure that the girls receiving first communion be dressed in the traditional white. Mam read it with a slight smile, then crumpled it and put it in her pocket.

'Your dress has arrived.' The blue dress lay on her bed, next to the old white one covered in plastic.

'Do you like it?' asked Mam. Ann shook her head, tears threatening.

'I honestly can't think what you see in Tricia's old dress,' Mam continued.

'It's white, it's the one I'm supposed to wear.'

Mam laughed softly. 'Blue is nicer on you, you look peaky in white.'

'I don't care, I want to wear this one.' She held the

white dress up close to her. 'I don't like that blue dress. I won't wear it.'

Footsteps came down the hall. Dad appeared over her shoulder.

'Now, now, that white doesn't suit you at all.'

Mam sniffed. 'After all my work this is the thanks I get.'

Dad looked at Ann and sighed, 'Now look what you've done, she's upset.'

Ann sat snivelling on the bed.

'Mam spent a lot of time and money, making sure you'd have a nice dress. That white dress is a tatty old thing.'

Ann bawled into the bedclothes.

'It's white,' she sobbed. How could she explain the image in her head, moving in white to the altar? The white dress had layers of faded lace, rows of pearl drops and buttons, even the crinkly feel of it moving against her fingers made her feel special. Who could feel holy in a turquoise dress with a sash of white daisies gathered at the waist?

'Why can't I wear the white one, why?'

Dad sighed. 'Look wear the blue one like a good girl. You want to be Daddy's girl, don't you?'

'I won't wear it, you want to make a holy show of me, I won't go at all.' She ran to where Mam sat in the dining room and shouted, 'I hate you, I hate you, I hate you.'

Mam said nothing. One hand was pressed to her forehead. Dad had come in behind Ann. He pulled her by the ear to the armchair.

'Now you see what I've to put up with, Sean?'

'How dare you speak to your mother like that! I won't have it, do you hear?'

Ann looked at him.

'Apologize and say you're sorry, apologize to your mother now.'

'No, I won't.'

'Right then.' He placed her over his knee. 'Take that and that, that'll teach you to have manners.'

'Go easy on her, Sean, don't hurt her.'

Ann kicked and squirmed as the slaps hailed her bottom and she was ejected out the back door.

'You're not getting back in here until you apologize.'

Ann stood on the step hiccupping and crying. It still wasn't dinner-time. She kicked and punched the back door for a while. Her nose dribbled and she began to get a headache. Mam came to the window, smiled and waved out at her. Ann stuck out her tongue and walked to the side of the house, where she couldn't be seen.

They marched two by two to the church, holding hands. As a class, they had never been outside the school yard before. The sounds and smells delighted and frightened them. It was market day and the squeal of the pigs, the smell of the cow-dung and the sharp 'hup, hup' voices of farmers filled the air. Pair by pair they were hustled into the dark empty church. Two confessional boxes were available; the class filled six rows. The first two rows had to kneel and repent, the others could sit back until their turns came. Ann couldn't decide which of her sins to put first: she told lies, she stole, and she was disobedient. The door opened and she was nudged forward. It was completely dark. A metal grid faced her, perforated with tiny holes. It was the same black darkness as the ghost trains in Bray; she wouldn't have been surprised if a skeleton brushed past her. The shutter was pulled back, with a clattering noise.

'This is your first confession, child?'

'Yes, Father, I confess to Almighty God and to you, Father.'

His profile leaned towards her, one hand over his eyes. It was the Monsignor.

'And tell me, what sins do you wish to confess?'

'I told lies, I stole, I was disobedient, that's all, Father.'

'These are all little sins, but if we don't try to curb them while we're young, they can lead to greater temptations. Now, who were you disobedient to?'

'To my mother, Father,' said Ann, thinking of the dress.

'For your penance say the act of contrition.' He gabbled through her absolution in Latin and made the sign of the cross,

'Go in peace.'

The shutter drew across and Ann was left in complete darkness. She leant all her weight against the door and it opened suddenly. She stood in the aisle blinking, before being shuttled into a pew. Through slits in her fingers, Ann watched Annette Daly walk down the main aisle, to the cordoned-off block of pews reserved for the class on Saturday. She shivered at the thought of the blue dress.

'Oh, my God, I am heartily sorry for all my sins.'

'Up, up, it's time to get up!' Dad shook her hurriedly, his back disappearing through the open doorway.

Turning on her side, she saw the dress covered in plastic hanging from the outside of the wardrobe. Piled in little mounds on the dressing table were the soft heap of white socks, knickers, vest and slip. A long, rectangular white cardboard box at the end of the bed contained her veil. Curlers dug into her scalp, especially where her head lay on the pillow.

'Do I have to call you again, Ann?' his voice came, from further down the hall.

'No, Dad, I'm up now,' her voice shouted back easily, as she lay on her back and stretched.

'Are you not dressed yet?' Mam watched her from the doorway.

'Will you take these out?' Ann sat in front of the dresser, pulling at the curlers. Mam quickly undid them and Ann's hair fell down like unfinished rope. As Mam used her forefinger and brush, large sausage ringlets appeared that bounced on either side of Ann's head. Mam parted the hair in the middle, then looped the ringlets back from her face with clips.

'There, you look lovely.'

Ann's hair felt strange and light, the ringlets tickled her cheeks and neck. Her fingers squashed one, it was quite soft yet kept its shape, she hated them. The dress hung glittering behind the plastic. Cold lining clung to her skin, as she stepped into it. She had said the rosary every night for the past month to save her from this moment, but it was no use. In the kitchen Tricia stopped spooning her cornflakes and stared at her.

'You look a sight.'

Ann made a face, and sat down pushing dry cereal around her bowl. Dad's head appeared in the door.

'Get a move on, or we'll never get there.'

In the hall, Mam fussed over the veil. She placed it over the ringlets with clips.

'I'll fix it better in the car.'

White gloves and a black handbag were thrust into her hands. She sat in the car motionless. Either there was a God or there wasn't. If there was he would stop this right now; if there wasn't, well at least she'd know. Mam turned around in the front and threw holy water over them as Dad revved the engine and reversed the car out the gate. Everything familiar flashed past. Her hands and armpits sweated as the car went faster and faster. Suddenly a dark shape hit the windscreen and slumped on to the bonnet. Mam and Tricia screamed, the car wavered and screeched to a halt. Blood and feathers hung congealed on the windscreen. Mam and Tricia turned their tear-stained faces at Dad.

'Damn and blast, are we ever going to get anywhere on time? It's only a bird for Christ's sake, Kate, a bloody bird.'

Mam sniffed into her handkerchief.

'We got a fright, that's all.'

Dad opened the door, Mam pushed a wad of tissues at him, 'In case of germs.'

He accepted them impatiently. He caught the dead bird by the wing, walked over to the ditch and dropped it.

'Say a prayer we won't have any more trouble,' said Mam.

Ann hugged herself with glee, she'd be too late to attend the ceremony now. He drove slowly the rest of the way to town, straining his neck to see the road clearly. He dropped them off at the side entrance. The church was crowded, with people standing three deep in the aisles. Ann was squashed into a seat beside two old men. The priest stood, hands outstretched at the offertory. The middle of the church was divided into black and white, boys and girls. Girls began to float to the altar, like dandelion puffs, and walked back, right past the block where Ann sat. She bent down further behind the man in front, and kept her hands over her face. Mary Sherlock was the first to appear, her eyes round and solemn, her hands joined under her nose. Sr. Ignatius stood near the altar, directing the traffic. Dad motioned her to move. The hymn being sung by the choir seemed to gather momentum as the sound swept forward.

> *'Ga-ther round*
> *the table of the Lord,*
> *eat his bod-y,*
> *drink his blood,*
> *and we'll sing a song of Love.'*

She walked to the altar behind the last of the stragglers. As she got nearer, her legs trembled, blood thudded in her ears. She kept her eyes glued to her joined hands as she crossed to kneel. The sway and tremble of the altar boy's smock came closer and closer. A salver was placed under her mouth. She held out her tongue and felt a disc as light as a feather laid there. As she turned to walk back, she caught the full horrified stare of Sr. Ignatius. The thought of swallowing the feather almost made her retch. She hurried back to her seat, almost running. Placing the white handkerchief Mam had given her in her hands, she knelt, and spat the host into it.

'Mass is ended, go in peace.'

At once, people clogged the narrow doors. Someone jabbed her shoulder sharply. 'I want to talk to you, miss.'

Dad smiled and nodded encouragingly to her. Ann followed the nun, up the empty centre of the church, past the altar and into the sacristy.

'Now I want to know what is the meaning of this?' Sr. Ignatius said pointing to the dress. Ann stared at her hands.

'Did you not give that note to your mother? How dare you attempt to receive a sacrament in that thing, and look at me when I'm speaking to you. This isn't the last you'll hear of this. Oh, I've seen many straps like you in my day and I know who you model yourselves on, not our Blessed Mother Mary, oh no, on Mary Magdalene, a fancy woman, making your first communion in blue!'

Ann heard herself say,

'It's not blue, it's turquoise.'

The nun watched her, her face as stiff as cardboard.

'Get out, get out of my sight.'

Ann shot out the side door and ran around the front. Mam and Dad stood in a huddle with other parents near the gates. While he was talking to Mr

Sherlock, Dad placed his hand on her head, pressing
the crown of flowers into her scalp, his other hand
held her bag and gloves. As they walked to the car,
Mam asked,

'Well, how did you like it?'

'Sr. Ignatius said I was like Mary Magdalene in this
dress,' Ann said.

'Did she now?' said Mam, smiling, amused by this.
'You look very nice in it, all the same, turquoise suits
you.'

Tricia stood at the car, smirking, then she hissed,
'You've got to get your photo taken yet, and you've
got to go around and visit people.'

Mam sat in the front dabbing perfume behind her
ears. As Dad started the car, she said, 'You know,
Sean, this town may have possibilities after all.'

'Is that so?' he said, turning down the main street.

Jack Gannon stood at Gorry's newsagents with his
cronies. A dog trailed in front of the car, its tail
swinging widely.

'Where to first?' he asked.

'I think we'll celebrate,' said Mam. 'Go to McGinn's
Hotel.'

Ann kicked at the seat in front of her, scuffing her
new, black patent shoes.

'I'm going to have it out with you tonight, God,
you and me are finished,' she promised.

Dotheboys Hall

CHARLES DICKENS

I couldn't consider a collection of school stories and extracts to be satisfying if it didn't include one of the most famous school scenes ever to appear in fiction. It is said that Charles Dickens' chief purpose in writing *Nicholas Nickleby*, from which the scene comes, was to show for the evil places they were the private schools which had sprung up in the 1820s and 1830s. He wanted readers to think about the 'monstrous neglect of education in England' at the time. In the scene which follows, the misery of the boys boarding at Dotheboys Hall is easily imagined. And should anyone accuse Dickens of exaggeration, think of those children in recent years who have been abused by those whose job it was to look after them.

Nicholas, taken on as an assistant master by
the school's proprietor and headmaster Wack-
ford Squeers, had dreamed of teaching young
noblemen in a grand mansion in Yorkshire.
What he discovers sickens him, and he eventually sides with the sad, lame and simple Smike
to defy the wicked regime.

Nicholas Nickleby was first published in 1839,
but the language strikes as hot and as cold as
today's light.

A ride of two hundred and odd miles in severe
weather, is one of the best softeners of a hard
bed that ingenuity can devise. Perhaps it is even a
sweetener of dreams, for those which hovered over
the rough couch of Nicholas and whispered their airy
nothings in his ear, were of an agreeable and happy
kind. He was making his fortune very fast indeed,
when the faint glimmer of an expiring candle shone
before his eyes, and a voice he had no difficulty in
recognizing as part and parcel of Mr Squeers, admon-
ished him that it was time to rise.

'Past seven, Nickleby,' said Mr Squeers.

'Has morning come already?' asked Nicholas, sitting
up in bed.

'Ah! that it has,' replied Squeers, 'and ready-
iced too. Now, Nickleby, come; tumble up, will
you?'

Nicholas needed no further admonition, but 'tumbled up' at once, and proceeded to dress himself by the light of the taper, which Mr Squeers carried in his hand.

'Here's a pretty go,' said that gentleman; 'the pump's froze.'

'Indeed!' said Nicholas, not much interested in the intelligence.

'Yes,' replied Squeers. 'You can't wash yourself this morning.'

'Not wash myself!' exclaimed Nicholas.

'No, not a bit of it,' rejoined Squeers tartly. 'So you must be content with giving yourself a dry polish till we break the ice in the well, and can get a bucketful out for the boys. Don't stand staring at me, but do look sharp, will you?'

Offering no further observation, Nicholas huddled on his clothes. Squeers, meanwhile, opened the shutters and blew the candle out; when the voice of his amiable consort was heard in the passage, demanding admittance.

'Come in, my love,' said Squeers.

Mrs Squeers came in, still habited in the primitive night-jacket which had displayed the symmetry of her figure on the previous night, and further ornamented with a beaver bonnet of some antiquity, which she wore, with much ease and lightness, on the top of the nightcap before mentioned.

'Drat the things,' said the lady, opening the cupboard; 'I can't find the school spoon anywhere.'

'Never mind it, my dear,' observed Squeers in a soothing manner; 'it's of no consequence.'

'No consequence, why how you talk!' retorted Mrs Squeers sharply. 'Isn't it brimstone morning?'

'I forgot, my dear,' rejoined Squeers; 'yes, it certainly is. We purify the boys' bloods now and then, Nickleby.'

'Purify fiddlesticks' ends,' said his lady. 'Don't think, young man, that we go to the expense of flower of brimstone and molasses just to purify them; because if you think we carry on the business in that way, you'll find yourself mistaken, and so I tell you plainly.'

'My dear,' said Squeers frowning. 'Hem!'

'Oh! nonsense,' rejoined Mrs Squeers. 'If the young man comes to be a teacher here, let him understand, at once, that we don't want any foolery about the boys. They have the brimstone and treacle, partly because if they hadn't something or other in the way of medicine they'd be always ailing and giving a world of trouble, and partly because it spoils their appetites and comes cheaper than breakfast and dinner. So, it does them good and us good at the same time, and that's fair enough I'm sure.'

Having given this explanation, Mrs Squeers put her hand into the closet and instituted a stricter search after the spoon, in which Mr Squeers assisted. A few words passed between them while they were thus engaged, but as their voices were partially stifled by the cupboard, all that Nicholas could distinguish was, that Mr Squeers said what Mrs Squeers had said was injudicious, and that Mrs Squeers said what Mr Squeers said was 'stuff'.

A vast deal of searching and rummaging ensued and, it proving fruitless, Smike was called in, and pushed by Mrs Squeers, and boxed by Mr Squeers, which course of treatment brightening his intellects, enabled him to suggest that possibly Mrs Squeers might have the spoon in her pocket, as indeed turned out to be the case. As Mrs Squeers had previously protested, however, that she was quite certain she had not got it, Smike received another box on the ear for presuming to contradict his mistress, together with a promise of a sound thrashing if he were not more respectful in future; so that he took nothing very advantageous by his motion.

'A most invaluable woman, that, Nickleby,' said Squeers when his consort had hurried away, pushing the drudge before her.

'Indeed, sir!' observed Nicholas.

'I don't know her equal,' said Squeers; 'I do not know her equal. That woman, Nickleby, is always the same – always the same bustling, lively, active, saving creetur that you see her now.'

Nicholas sighed involuntarily at the thought of the agreeable domestic prospect thus opened to him; but Squeers was, fortunately, too much occupied with his own reflections to perceive it.

'It's my way to say, when I am up in London,' continued Squeers, 'that to them boys she is a mother. But she is more than a mother to them; ten times more. She does things for them boys, Nickleby, that I don't believe half the mothers going would do for their own sons.'

'I should think they would not, sir,' answered Nicholas.

Now, the fact was, that both Mr and Mrs Squeers viewed the boys in the light of their proper and natural enemies; or, in other words, they held and considered that their business and profession was to get as much from every boy as could by possibility be screwed out of him. On this point they were both agreed, and behaved in unison accordingly. The only difference between them was, that Mrs Squeers waged war against the enemy openly and fearlessly, and that Squeers covered his rascality, even at home, with a spice of his habitual deceit; as if he really had a notion of some day or other being able to take himself in, and persuade his own mind that he was a very good fellow.

'But come,' said Squeers, interrupting the progress of some thoughts to this effect in the mind of his usher, 'let's go to the schoolroom; and lend me a hand with my school coat, will you?'

Nicholas assisted his master to put on an old fustian shooting-jacket, which he took down from a peg in the passage; and Squeers, arming himself with his cane, led the way across a yard, to a door in the rear of the house.

'There,' said the schoolmaster as they stepped in together; 'this is our shop, Nickleby!'

It was such a crowded scene, and there were so many objects to attract attention, that, at first, Nicholas stared about him, really without seeing anything at all. By degrees, however, the place resolved itself into a bare and dirty room, with a couple of windows, whereof a tenth part might be of glass, the remainder being stopped up with old copy-books and paper. There were a couple of long old rickety desks, cut and notched, and inked, and damaged, in every possible way; two or three forms; a detached desk for Squeers; and another for his assistant. The ceiling was supported, like that of a barn, by cross-beams and rafters; and the walls were so stained and discoloured that it was impossible to tell whether they had ever been touched with paint or whitewash.

But the pupils – the young noblemen! How the last faint traces of hope, the remotest glimmering of any good to be derived from his efforts in this den, faded from the mind of Nicholas as he looked in dismay around! Pale and haggard faces, lank and bony figures, children with the countenances of old men, deformities with irons upon their limbs, boys of stunted growth, and others whose long meagre legs would hardly bear their stooping bodies, all crowded on the view together. There were little faces which should have been handsome, darkened with the scowl of sullen, dogged suffering; there was childhood with the light of its eye quenched, its beauty gone, and its helplessness alone remaining; there were vicious-faced boys, brooding, with leaden eyes, like malefactors in a jail.

And yet this scene, painful as it was, had its grotesque features, which, in a less interested observer than Nicholas, might have provoked a smile. Mrs Squeers stood at one of the desks, presiding over an immense basin of brimstone and treacle, of which delicious compound she administered a large instalment to each boy in succession: using for the purpose a common wooden spoon, which might have been originally manufactured for some gigantic top, and which widened every young gentleman's mouth considerably: they being all obliged, under heavy corporal penalties, to take in the whole of the bowl at a gasp. In another corner, huddled together for companionship, were the little boys who had arrived on the preceding night, three of them in very large leather breeches, and two in old trousers, a something tighter fit than drawers are usually worn; at no great distance from these was seated the juvenile son and heir of Mr Squeers – a striking likeness of his father – kicking, with great vigour, under the hands of Smike, who was fitting upon him a pair of new boots that bore a most suspicious resemblance to those which the least of the little boys had worn on the journey down – as the little boy himself seemed to think, for he was regarding the appropriation with a look of most rueful amazement. Besides these, there was a long row of boys waiting, with countenances of no pleasant anticipation, to be treacled; and another file, who had just escaped from the infliction, making a variety of wry mouths indicative of anything but satisfaction. The whole were attired in such motley, ill-sorted, extraordinary garments, as would have been irresistibly ridiculous, but for the foul appearance of dirt, disorder, and disease, with which they were associated.

'Now,' said Squeers, giving the desk a great rap with his cane, which made half the little boys nearly jump out of their boots, 'is that physicking over?'

'Just over,' said Mrs Squeers, choking the last boy in her hurry, and tapping the crown of his head with the wooden spoon to restore him. 'Here, you Smike; take away now. Look sharp!'

Smike shuffled out with the basin, and Mrs Squeers, having called up a little boy with a curly head and wiped her hands upon it, hurried out after him into a species of wash-house, where there was a small fire and a large kettle, together with a number of little wooden bowls which were arranged upon a board.

Into these bowls, Mrs Squeers, assisted by the hungry servant, poured a brown composition which looked like diluted pincushions without the covers, and was called porridge. A minute wedge of brown bread was inserted in each bowl, and when they had eaten their porridge by means of the bread, the boys ate the bread itself, and had finished their breakfast; whereupon Mr Squeers said, in a solemn voice, 'For what we have received, may the Lord make us truly thankful!' – and went away to his own.

Nicholas distended his stomach with a bowl of porridge, for much the same reason which induces some savages to swallow earth – lest they should be inconveniently hungry when there is nothing to eat. Having further disposed of a slice of bread and butter, allotted to him in virtue of his office, he sat himself down to wait for school-time.

He could not but observe how silent and sad the boys all seemed to be. There was none of the noise and clamour of a schoolroom; none of its boisterous play, or hearty mirth. The children sat crouching together, and shivering together, and seemed to lack the spirit to move about. The only pupil who evinced the slightest tendency towards locomotion or playfulness was Master Squeers, and as his chief amusement was to tread upon the other boys' toes in his new boots, his flow of spirits was rather disagreeable than otherwise.

After some half-hour's delay, Mr Squeers re-appeared, and the boys took their places and their books, of which latter commodity the average might be about one to eight learners. A few minutes having elapsed, during which Mr Squeers looked very profound, as if he had a perfect apprehension of what was inside all the books, and could say every word of their contents by heart if he only chose to take the trouble, that gentleman called up the first class.

Obedient to this summons there ranged themselves in front of the schoolmaster's desk, half a dozen scarecrows, out at knees and elbows, one of whom placed a torn and filthy book beneath his learned eye.

'This is the first class in English spelling and philosophy, Nickleby,' said Squeers, beckoning Nicholas to stand beside him. 'We'll get up a Latin one, and hand that over to you. Now then, where's the first boy?'

'Please, sir, he's cleaning the back parlour window,' said the temporary head of the philosophical class.

'So he is, to be sure,' rejoined Squeers. 'We go upon the practical mode of teaching, Nickleby; the regular education system. C-l-e-a-n, clean, verb active, to make bright, to scour. W-i-n, win, d-e-r, der, winder, a casement. When the boy knows this out of the book, he goes and does it. It's just the same principle as the use of the globes. Where's the second boy?'

'Please, sir, he's weeding the garden,' replied a small voice.

'To be sure,' said Squeers, by no means disconcerted. 'So he is. B-o-t, bot, t-i-n, tin, bottin, n-e-y, ney, bottinney, noun substantive, a knowledge of plants. When he has learned that bottinney means a knowledge of plants, he goes and knows 'em. That's our system, Nickleby; what do you think of it?'

'It's a very useful one, at any rate,' answered Nicholas.

'I believe you,' rejoined Squeers, not remarking the emphasis of his usher. 'Third boy, what's a horse?'

'A beast, sir,' replied the boy.

'So it is,' said Squeers. 'Ain't it, Nickleby?'

'I believe there is no doubt of that, sir,' answered Nicholas.

'Of course there isn't,' said Squeers. 'A horse is a quadruped, and quadruped's Latin for beast, as everybody that's gone through the grammar knows, or else where's the use of having grammars at all?'

'Where, indeed!' said Nicholas abstractedly.

'As you're perfect in that,' resumed Squeers, turning to the boy, 'go and look after *my* horse, and rub him down well, or I'll rub you down. The rest of the class go and draw water up, till somebody tells you to leave off, for it's washing-day tomorrow, and they want the coppers filled.'

So saying, he dismissed the first class to their experiments in practical philosophy, and eyed Nicholas with a look, half cunning and half doubtful, as if he were not altogether certain what he might think of him by this time.

'That's the way we do it, Nickleby,' he said, after a pause.

Nicholas shrugged his shoulders in a manner that was scarcely perceptible, and said he saw it was.

'And a very good way it is, too,' said Squeers. 'Now, just take them fourteen little boys, and hear them some reading, because, you know, you must begin to be useful. Idling about here won't do.'

Mr Squeers said this, as if it had suddenly occurred to him, either that he must not say too much to his assistant, or that his assistant did not say enough to him in praise of the establishment. The children were arranged in a semicircle round the new master, and he was soon listening to their dull, drawling, hesitating recital of those stories of engrossing interest which are to be found in the more antiquated spelling books.

In this exciting occupation, the morning lagged heavily on. At one o'clock, the boys, having previously had their appetites thoroughly taken away by stir-about and potatoes, sat down in the kitchen to some hard salt beef, of which Nicholas was graciously permitted to take his portion to his own solitary desk, to eat it there in peace. After this, there was another hour of crouching in the schoolroom and shivering with cold, and then school began again.

Acknowledgements

The editor and publishers gratefully acknowledge the following for permission to reproduce copyright material in this anthology in the form of complete stories and extracts taken from the following books:

Sally Cinderella by Bernard Ashley published by Orchard Books, London, copyright © Bernard Ashley 1989; 'The Mouth-organ Boys' from *A Thief in the Village* by James Berry published by Hamish Hamilton Children's Books, copyright © James Berry 1987; 'First Communion' from *School Daze* by Ger Duffy published by Sheba, copyright © Ger Duffy 1990; *The Boy from New York City* by Marcel Feigel, copyright © Marcel Feigel 1992; 'The Mile' from *A Northern Childhood* by George Layton from Sky Books Series published by Longman Group UK Ltd, copyright © George Layton 1978; 'The Choice is Yours' from *Nothing to be Afraid Of* by Jan Mark published by Viking Kestrel, copyright © Jan Mark 1980; 'Jam for Bunter!' from *Billy Bunter of Greyfriars School* by Frank Richards first published by Charles Skilton, copyright © Una Hamilton-Wright, permission granted by Tessa Sayle Agency; 'Madame Fidolia and the Dancing Class' from *Ballet Shoes* by Noel Streatfeild published by J. M. Dent & Sons Ltd, copyright © Noel Streatfeild 1936.